L.O.V.E.

Lust that Overwhelms the Value of Emotions, Volume 1

Im Him

Published by IM HIM LLC., 2023.

L.O.V.E.

First edition. January 11, 2023.

ISBN: 979-8215744499

Written by Im Him.

Dedication

Hey Hey whats goin on beautiful people. I'd like to take this moment to thank everyone who's taken a chance reading my book. I definitely wanna give ah big shoutout to my "Charlie's Angle" team that's helped along the way and to everyone who has been on my head about getting this story out to everyone. This is the first of many accomplishments to come from me and my team, I'm just thankful that the ones that are still here didn't give up on me.

I love yall,

I'm Him

* **Be sure to follow me on TicTok, tag me in a review I'd love to hear what you guys think.**

-313imhim

-TheeEdibleTeddyBear

L.O.V.E.

(Lust that Overwhelms the Value of Emotions)
Love is a blinding word... When those three words "I Love You" come together. It's supposed to be coming from the heart... Love can make you feel sad and misused... But love can also make
you feel like the most valuable person on the face of this earth... As humans we are bound to make mistakes and fall under false presences of what love really is... But each mistake is a learning experience... And with each learning experience... It opens a new chapter in your life... Love is a word that should never be used in vain, but once again we are human and the most common misconception of what love truly stands for... Is... Sex. It will only be a few times in your life where you will encounter true love... And most of the time you won't even know it because you are so caught up in physical features...The rest of your life is pure lust... It starts to become a continuous three-way battle between your mind, your body, and your heart... If you follow the right one you gain a Soulmate and a life of happiness... While following the wrong one will only lead to heartbreaks, headaches, and a life constantly
questioning yourself, wondering if you are worth a life of happiness... Every man and every woman deserves an opportunity to love and be loved... The problem is... We treat love like a game, so, you either play or get Played...

L.A.'s Story......

Growing up there was always a part of me that I felt was missing

after I lost my father. Well, my father was more so taken away from

me at a young age. He was gunned down in front of me all over a dice

game. I have yet to find the mutha fucker's that killed him, but trust

me, I'm not done looking. After my father was murdered growing up

with my OG was hard, the older I got the less

I saw her. It wasn't her fault though. She was working two jobs busting her ass every day to provide for both of us. It was hard watching my mother struggle to keep a roof over our head's and keep her son happy and give me what she didn't have coming up. The older I got the more tired I grew seeing my mother struggle. My OG raised me to be a man the best way she could, but it was some things as a man I had to learn on my own; like how to provide. I was too young to get a job so at the age of sixteen I turned to the streets. I started rolling and before I turned eighteen I had my own house, three cars: a 2004 dark blue Ford Mustang, a 2006 black on black fully loaded Escalade, and a new 2008 Jeep Commander. I even moved my OG out of the city. At the time I was rolling for one of the biggest drug dealers in the city. They called him Duce...Why? Well from what I hear it's because there are only two things that he cared about, his family and his money. I met Duce through a childhood friend of mine named James Derrick, but we call him Bossman. Bossman and I lived next door to each other most of my life. He was a few year older than me but I was always mature for my age. We weren't as close back then as we are now. We became like brothers, unbreakable after one day I was walking home from school about two years ago, and in was getting robbed about two blocks away from my house. Bossman just happened to be walking up the side street right in front of me. That was a moment I would never forget. Two guys ran up on me with bandanas covering their faces...

"A little nigga run ya pockets!" the guy with the gun demanded. Mind you I have never been robbed before, let alone have I ever stared down the barrel of a gun. I was stuck as the other guy walked up to me going through my pockets...

"Don't move" the deep voice behind the bandana called out. Next thing you know two shots echo out through the streets. I thought for a split second I was dead as I dropped to the ground and I see Bossman aiming a 357 at the thugs that were robbing me. He let off two more shots that sent the thugs running in the other direction.

"Ah... man you, okay?" he asked as he reached out a hand helping me to my feet.

"Yea, yea I'm good, thanks for stepping in." I said.

"I had to man, it's not safe out here." he responded.

After that we got to know each other over the years. I got to know his mother, and his sister Monique. Before I knew she was his sister I had the biggest crush on Monique. Shit I still do, but Bossman is my boy, so you know she was off limits. The closer Bossman and I got the more I saw that our stories were damn near the same. He grew up with a father that walked out on him, his sister and his mother. Our struggles were so similar I believe that's why we have managed to stay so close ever since. Bossman plugging me with Duce was far from a problem. He let me know off rip though that Duce was not a guy to be fucked with, period. When Duce put me on my first sack his exact words to me was...

"This is a grown man's game son, you sure you ready to play it?". It felt like I

was giving my soul over to the devil, but at the time all I could think about is making things easier on my OG...

" Yea, yea I'm ready." I answered. When I started rolling, I quickly became "that guy" both in the streets and in school. My mother always told me" If you don't do school, you don't do nothing.", so even though I was out hustling I stayed in school because I knew one day getting an education would pay off. Plus, it made my OG happy, outside of my voice of course. Every time I sang I would always see her glow and she would always say" Son, you have the voice of an Angel.". I would always think she was just saying that because she was my mother, but it was the truth. It was just a talent that I didn't tap into until a few years later. Over my Freshman, Sophomore, and Jr years I built up a reputation for myself not just in the drug game but seducing the ladies in my school as well as others outside my school with my voice. I'm not sure if it was the swag, the money, cars, or my voice that had the ladies chosen; all I know is something was working. I had all of them breaking them necks to be with me, everyone except Monique. She didn't seem to be mesmerized by my lifestyle and all the materialistic shit. She was the only girl I would have taken seriously, but when she went off to college, I gave up hope; oh, and the fact that Bossman is my boy played a part as well. Other than her I never took any girl in my school serious because all of them were just money hungry. So, I just played the role fuck and leave. I can't lie I was a dog that is until my senior year when I met this girl named Jackie. Jackie stood about five foot three, so she was short enough for me to look down at. She was a soft caramel apple tone, and just as sweet. She had soft warm lips that have you ready to melt from just one kiss, hazel eyes that make you

just forget about all your problems, and a smile that could light up a room. Thick, about 210 EASY, with a coke bottle figure, and trust me, very well proportioned.

The Lock-In.......

*B*ossman and I was going to a lock-in-party. I was just getting home

from picking up my Letterman's jacket from the mall at the LV outlet.

As soon as I stopped inside the door my phone goes off. It took me a few

minutes to answer it because I had to put all my bags down. I catch

the last ring before it went to voice mail...

"Hello?" I answered.

"L.A., man you ready for this lock-in party tonight?" Bossman asked.

"Hell yea, you know I just grabbed me a new fit. Ya boy gone be LV
from head to toe" I said.

"Boy you out here getting too much money." Bossman jokingly said.
Which was a true statement. Between the two of us I was the only one
flipping eight keys a week...

"Yea fool and speaking of money, you still got my shades?" I asked. A
few days ago, Bossman and I went out to the strip club, and he wanted
to sport my Buffs, so us being boys I let him. I had just forgot to grab
them from him that night...

"Yea I gott'em." he said.

"Good, I'm gonna need them tonight to top off this fit." I told him.

"That's cool man...hey...I need you to scoop me up tonight." Bossman
said. A moment of silence flowed through the air. I couldn't figure out
why he wanted me to pick him up when he has a car...

6

"Alright man. I'm bouta hit the shower and get dressed." I replied. "Alright cool, just scoop me up at eight o'clock tonight." he said. I glanced over at the clock mounted on the living room wall. Its already 5:35p.m.

"Alright my guy. Make sure you ready fool." I told him. He gave a bit of a chuckle as he ended the convo knowing that he is always late...

"Alright One." Bossman said before hanging up.

"One." I replied before I hung up the phone. I took my clothes out of the bag and layer them out on the bed then I hopped into the shower. By the time I got out it's about 7:00 pm. I threw on my new fit and walked over to the dresser. Looking into the mirror as I threw on my black triple plated Shinola, I fixed the collar of my button-down, before fastening my LV belt, then slid my feet into my LV loafers. As I take my time and get dressed, I happened to glance down at my watch and it's ten minutes to eight. I go to the front room and throw on my LV Letterman's jacket. I grab my phone, wallet, and my keys off the kitchen table and then made my way out the front door.

"Hey L.A.!" a voice called out from a short distance. I turned around and see it's my neighbor Lisa. Lisa moved in about a month after me. I don't know much about her. All I know is she's twenty-five years old, about five foot seven, brown skinned, no kids, and her body was nicely shaped. She's been hitting on me since she got here, or at least I think so. I haven't shot my shot yet...

"Hey Lisa, how you doing today?" I asked. She swiftly made her way over to my side of the street meeting me in front of my car...

"I'm good...you looking damn good" she replied as I leaned on the hood of my car, "where you headed Mr.?" she asked. Before answering I noticed that she had on this long baby blue silk, pajama dress that that fit her to the curve. When her robe loosened, I could see that she didn't have on a bra the way her nipples stuck out from the lining of her tight dress, which then made me question whether she was wearing any panties...

"Shit, just heading out to this lock-in party. It's a fundraiser for this youth home on the westside"I said.

"Oh okay, that sounds like it should be some fun." she replied while following me over to my car door. As I opened it...

"Yea, I hope so." I said. She stepped a little closer and fixed the collar of my jacket...

"Well I'm not going to hold you up." she said while leaning in for a hug. I can tell by the immediate second breath that she took taking in the scent of my Polo Black cologne that she was possibly turned on by the aroma. I felt a slight kiss on my neck, then whispered in my ear. "Be safe." she said. I was a little confused by the gesture. As she walked away, I slid into my seat closed the door, reeved up the engine and pulled off. I pulled up to Bossman's place in the black '08 Jeep Commander with the 5% tint sitting on dubs. He hops in...

"Daaamn boy when you pick this up?" He asked.

"Shit I just got about two weeks ago." I replied. He started helplessly saying with the different compartments...

"This bitch is nice boy!" he exclaimed.

"Thanks—-" I said. Hesitating, with a hint of curiosity in my voice I continued..."Where is yo ride at anyway?" I asked. He slumped down in the seat as if he was disappointed...

"Shit in the shop." he replied.

"What! Why? you just got it!" I said. Bossman shrugged his shoulders...

"Yea, I know man. I call myself being nice and I let my OG use it to go to her doctor's appointment a few days ago, and on her way home she hit a pothole and snapped the axel in half." he replied.

"Damn, she okay though?" I asked. He knew my question was sincere, but he must have sensed me trying to hold back a smile, which I was. His OG cannot drive.

"Yea, her ass just ain't driving my shit no more." he said. We both laughed out loud...

"*Now you know how many cars ya OG den ran through. She can't drive.*" *I said joking. Joining in with my teasing he responded...*
"*I know man, she done totaled three cars this year already.*" *he proclaimed. We both continue laughing...*"*L.A., man I know you got some sounds in this bitch.*" *he said. He was so used to me having the best sounds in the city in my cars...*
"*Nah, I don't but the original stereo kick good.*" *I said. I popped in one of my mixed CDs, cranked it up a little, and we banged the CD out until we got to the lock-in. We pulled up and we see ladies everywhere walking across the parking lot. All different shapes, sizes, skin tones, and a lot of them were wearing those all-purpose dresses. That's one of those dresses that you can go out to a formal affair in and come home and go right to happy hour. A group of ladies standing by the doorway entrance waving spoke...*
"*Hey L.A.! Hey Bossman!*" *they said.*
"*Hey ladies!*" *we both responded together. Bossman and I stepped into the building, and I can't lie, the set up was nice. They had balloons all over the wall and ceiling. Decorations from top to bottom with bright colors and the DJ was mixing his ass off. Bossman heard the* "*Cha Cha Slide*" *playing through the speakers and he immediately went right to the dance floor. See, he was more of a party animal than I was, but I still knew how to enjoy myself. I started to mingle with a few people that knew me from school and around the hood. As I was watching everyone out on the dance floor enjoying themselves something told me to look to my right. There she was. My eyes were instantly placed on an Angel. She was sitting over by the bar. She had on this short black dress that barely cover just enough of her legs to hold some mystery. I knew I had to have her. Her back was facing me when I walked over to her. My hands softly grazed across her milk chocolate skin...*
"*Hey beautiful.*" *I said. She turned and looked at me , then like a swift breeze she resumed her original position. Even though she blew me off*

I couldn't give up. I could tell she was not having a good night, but I was determined to change that. After I gathered my thoughts all of my thoughts I pulled out a stool and sat next to her. She looked at me in my eyes as if I was lost..."Hey beautiful, how are you?" I asked I gave a slight pause just in case she responded, but she didn't so I continued..."My name is Frank, but my friends call me L.A." I said. Now I'm not

sure what was going through my mind when I told her my real name. That's something I would never do because it was easier for me to remain a ghost with the ladies and never get caught up. When I started rolling everyone in the streets knew me as L.A. Only a very select few people knew my real name just in case some shit pops off and I must disappear. I detected a slight grin appear upon her beautiful face...

"Frank huh?" she asked sarcastically. She paused adjusting her body on the stool. "You don't look like a Frank." she said. We both shared a smile.

"So what exactly does a Frank look like?" I asked. She shrugged her shoulders before responding...

"I don't know, when I hear the name Frank, I just think old white guy with a potbelly or something. But you're the exact opposite of that. Tall, dark and handsome." she said...I can't lie, after that compliment started feeling myself...

"Can I get you something to drink?" I asked. She hesitated...

"Sure, nothing strong though, I do have to drive home." she said... Waving over to the waiter...

"Hey waiter, what is the lightest wine you got?" I asked.

"Arbor-Mist." he said. She nodded in in acceptance to that selection...

" That's fine, I'll take two glasses of that, one for me and one for Mrs....? I said and waited. A beautiful smile that lit up the room came across her face...

"Jackie. My name is Jackie." she said. I looked back over at the waiter...

"One for Mrs. Jackie" I said. I turned back to her reaching out for her hand...

"It's a pleasure to meet you L.A." Jackie said.

"No, the pleasure is all mine" I said. The waiter returned with the drinks. We both lifted our glasses as if for a formal toast. The China glass rang together...

"So, Mr. Frank" she said.

"Yes Mrs. Jackie?" I replied.

"Why do they call you L.A.?" she asked. I finished the sip of wine I was taking as she hit me with the question. I sat my glass down...

"Well they call me L.A. because I am a lyrical angel." I answered.

"So you rap?" she asked. The look on her face led me to believe that she had become a little less interested maybe thinking I was the typical wanna be...

"No, I Sing, and I rap. I'm a little multi-talented." I responded. A slight grin formed in the corners of her cheeks.

"Oh yeah? So—-", she places her hand on top of mine, "what other talents do you have?" she asked. She leaned in with curiosity. At first, I thought that it might have been the liquor in her system talking, but the I looked at her glass and realized that her glass was barely halfway empty. I sat up and leaned in close enough to whisper in her ear...

"Well that's for me to know and you to find out." I said. My finger slowly grazed across her soft cheeks as I spoke...

"I would like to find out." she said. She looked as if I was a lion, and she was begging me to take her as my prey. We both shared another sip of wine and sat out glasses down almost simultaneously. I then stood up and I took Jackie by her hand, and in a swift moment we found ourselves gliding onto the dance floor. In the process, ironically, the DJ was playing R Kelly's

"Step in the name of love"......"L.A. I.....I can't dance." she said shyly. She giggled as if she was embarrassed and placed her hands over her face. I gently grabbed her hands and placed them on my shoulders,

then I slowly wrapped my arms around her waist. I whispered in her ear...

"Just follow me and allow the music to flow through you." I said. Her arms locked in around my neck as she exhaled deeply relaxing her body. We began dancing. After a few songs we she looked up and leaned in...

"I see that you are a pretty good dancer." she said. We both smiled. We both enjoyed a few more songs and before we knew it we had danced the night away. We hear the volume of the music start to lower and the DJ makes an announcement...

"Ladies and Gentlemen this is the last song for the night, so take someone special by the hand and get to the dance floor." I looked down at her as she looked at me, and for a moment it was like our souls touched with our eyes. Even though we were inside a dim setting her skin, her beauty still seemed to glow. Everything slowed down. that moment seemed so perfect. Standing on her tippy toes she leaned in to kiss me. I came the rest of the distance and our lips touched. The taste of her warm, juicy lips masked in the flavor of strawberries had me completely stuck. She gave me the warmest feeling that I haven't had since Monique frfr left for college. The arch in her back grew deeper as her leg lifted off the floor. She even ended the kiss biting my bottom lip. I can tell she was feeling me. The song ended, and yet we still found ourselves in the center

of the dance floor. Still holding on to each other, we created some space between us. Interlocking hands I fixed my lips...

"What are your plans for tonight? I asked. She took a half step back before responding. I could tell by the look on her face that this wasn't going to be an easy one. Truthfully, I was hoping that she wasn't easy.

"L.A. listen, I have had very beautiful time with you tonight. You truly made my night. I would be lying if I said that I was not feeling you." she said. She softly placed her palms on my chest slowly working her way down to my abdomen..."Because lord knows I am but *unfortunately, I'm not that type of woman. I am sorry." she said. She turns to walk away, but before she could take a second step she found herself spun around and wrapped up in the grace of my arms...*

"Jackie...I can respect that." I said. I paused, slowly running my hand down the sides of her soft cheeks..."Listen, if I offended you in any way I apologize." I said sincerely. She smiled..."Could I give you a call tonight, Jackie?" I asked.

"Sure, I don't see any harm in that." she replied. I reached into my pocket and pulled out my phone and placed it in her hands. She went right to the dial pad and started putting her number, but before she put in her last four digits, she stopped..."You're not a stalker, are you?" she asked. I let out a light chuckle...

"It seems that you are a little discombobulated tonight. That's typically a question you ask before kissing them?" I said. We both smiled, and her cheeks blushed as she handed me back my phone. We made our way off the dance floor and over to the door. It was a nice night outside despite the slight chill in the air. I wrapped my Letterman's jacket around her shoulders as we slowly walked over to her car..."A black 1998 drop-top, Twin exhaust Mustang." I said impressed. She stepped back as if she was shocked...

"You know your cars I see." she said in response as we walked to the driver side. I noticed the pink and black leather interior...

"Yeah, I know a little something." I said. Before she got into the driver seat, we shared another warm hug followed by a kiss on the cheek...

"I'll be looking forward to your call L.A." she said. She slowly eased her door shut. She rolled down her window waiting for a response...

"Okay baby girl, it's going to a little late though. Give me at least an hour. I gotta drop my boy off at home." I spoke. In disbelief of me actually calling she replied stiffly...

"Mmhm...don't keep me waiting. "she said while folding her arms checking her watch...

"Trust me I won't." I said. I leaned in softly giving her that reassuring response. She leans out of the window and gibes me another kiss, then pulls off. As she slowly emerged from the parking spot she waved goodbye, I waved back. I try

calling Bossman's phone so we can leave. The quicker I get home the better chances I have of sweet-talking Jackie into coming over. Bossman's

phone kept going to voicemail, and I thought to myself "See, this is why we drive desperate. His ass always late on some bullshit. Moments later here comes Bossman with two little chicks on his arm...

"L.A. this is BB and Chrystal. Ladies this is my man L.A.." Bossman said.

"Hey L.A.." the ladies said together.

"Hey ladies, what's going on?" I said.

"L.A., man these ladies were wondering where the "after-party" was." he said. BB began to walk right up to with this long tight red dress with slits in the sides that traveled right up to her thighs. She leaned in and whispered into my ear...

"Guess what? "she said. In that same soft tone I ask...

"What's up?" I answered, and she reaches down, slowly cupping my dick in her hand...

"I like chocolate." she explained.

"Is that right? I asked in return. Well I can tell that my plans for tonight have changed. She nods in acceptance to my question...

"Now I know you are not going to make me beg for this...are you?" she said teasingly. Lightly she tugs at my ear with her teeth. I'm just thinking to myself "Hell naw I'm not!" but I played it cool until her soft lips touched my neck. After that it was over. I damn near melted, sending a burst of impulses from my neck down to my legs. I tried to fight it, but I gave in. When I finally gained my composer and fixed my lips to say...

"So you lookin for the after party huh?" I asked even though the question was rhetorical BB nodded her head while hitting her bottom lip. I walked her over to the passenger side as Bossman and Chrystal made their way to the car...
"Let's go!" I called out as all four of us got into my car. We pulled off. Bossman asked me to stop at the liqueur store up the street...
"L.A., man hit Pop's on the corner so I can grab me some drank." he said.
"Alright." I replied. I pulled up to the store. Leaving the car running...
"We'll be right back ladies.", Bossman and I walked into the store...
"What's going on Pops, you alright?" I asked...
"Yeah L.A. I'm hanging in there. How's your mama doing?" Pops asked. Bossman walked off to the back to grab him some pop and orange juice while I grabbed the liquor...
"She's alright Pops. Hey let me get a pint of cold Remy Martin VSOP." I said. Pops turned to reach into the refrigerator and grabbed the bottle and put it right inside a brown paper bag.
"What I owe you Pops?" I asked as I pulled out my money. Pops came from behind the glass placing his hands on top of mine...
"Son, you know that your money is no good here. Just be sure to tell your mother I said hello." he told me. See, Pops has been knowing my mother and father for a while. He's been helping my OG out ever since I could walk. I remember when I was about seven years old, he told me in front of my mother " As long as you keep this young lady happy, stay in school, and get good grades, you don't ever have to worry about paying for anything when you come here. You just tell me what you want and it's yours." He knew my father before he was murdered, and he used to always tell me what a great man my father was and how he saw that same potential in me; and ever since that day Pops has stuck to his word..."I'll tell her Pops." I said. Even though it was free I still left Pops sixty dollars on the counter and Bossman, and I left. We got back in the car and pulled off. The whole ride to drop Bossman

and Chrystal off BB is in the front seat with me grabbing and rubbing all over my dick while I'm playing with her wet, juicy pussy. I happen to have looked into my mirror and I see Chrystal's head bobbing up and down going nuts. I pull up to Bossman's driveway. Bossman and Chrystal both get out and Bossman comes over to my window, while Chrystal walked up to the front door looking back waving at BB...

"Alright L.A. man, y'all be good." he said as a devilish smile spread on his face as he spoke...

"Alright fool, hit me up in the morning." I replied. It was crazy that he said "be good" because as soon as I pulled out of the driveway BB positioned herself in the seat, slid over moving the armrest out of the way. Then she unzipped my pants and slowly pulled my dick out and kissed the tip. As I pulled off, she started slowly easing her warm juicy lips further and further down my dick. She came up for a brief moment running her tongue slowly across the tip of my shit...

"I wonder how many licks it will take to get to the creamy middle of this blow-pop." she said

playfully letting out a little giggle. She looked up at me with a smile of satisfaction while I watched her wrap her warm lips around my dick easing her way back down, until she had every inch of my dick inside of her throat. Now mind you I only live a few main streets down from Bossman place, so I'm trying my hardest not to crush this brand new mutha fucking car while she's sucking the skin off my dick. We finally make it to my house. I pull up in the driveway

and as soon as I put the car in park and shut the engine off. She starts getting sloppier with the head. I look down and my red Polo boxers are soaked. She gets on her knees in the seat and hikes up her dress all while my dicks lodged between her tonsils and esophagus. I start rubbing on her ass and her pussy playing with her clit through her panties. She slowly slides her lips off my dick while looking up at me. That shit almost drove me crazy. Then she starts kissing and sucking all over my neck. Once I leaned my seat back she hikes up her dress to the middle of her flat stomach, and she climbed on top of me. I moved her panties to the side as she slowly grabs my dick, rubs it against her clit, and then eases me inside of her wet, warm, throbbing pussy. She takes her time easing every inch inside of her. Then she places her hands on my chest as she slowly starts rocking back and forth. I let her take control and have little fun. I look down and all I see is her warm cum sliding down my dick. I then held her bottom half down while I gave her slow deep strokes causing her to sink her teeth into my neck deeper trying not to scream. I let her bust a few nuts, but now it was time for me to get a little more comfortable. I ease her up off of me. She pulled her dress down and I didn't bother fixing myself, it was dark who cares. I took her though the side door and as soon as I closed the door, she hops all over me kissing and sucking all over my neck. I carry her all the way over to the kitchen counter and I sit her on top of it. She starts to take my belt and pants off while I'm tossing my shirt and getting her out of her dress. I strip her down to just her pink laced panties and I start kissing her neck. Working my way down to her soft perky lil tities. I slowly drop down to one knee and wrap her legs around my neck as I start kissing her on her inner thighs, and it seems like the closer I get to her pussy the wetter she's getting. I sink my nails into her thighs and be gain devouring her pussy making sure not a drop of her strawberry tasting juices hit the floor. Then it crossed my mind that maybe the strawberry flavor I'm tasting might just be the lipstick Jackie had on, either way I'm loving it. I can tell by the way her legs are shaking and the way she's moaning and pulling my hair that she's getting ready to climax...

"Ahh! Oh my god L.A...ooo baby I'm about to cum!" she yelled. See, I told you. I come up and eased my dick inside of her and she let out a load moan of relief. I slowly started stroking back and forth while rubbing on her tities and playing with her clit. Next thing you know the strokes just become deeper, and deeper they are, the harder the

next stroke becomes. She starts having orgasms consecutively and each time harder than the last one. I finally get ready to cum...

"Damn baby girl I'm about to nut.... where you want it?" I asked.

"Mmmm daddy, I'm about to cum too. I want it all over my clit.." she moaned out. I watched as she bust all over my dick. Moments later I pulled out as slow as possible and nutted all over her stomach and just sat my dick there before sliding back in. Its making her jump feeling the pressure of my dick pulsating against her walls. She slides down off the counter and starts cleaning up the mess

she left all over my dick. When she was done...

"I'll be right back." she said as she shot to the restroom to clean herself up. Meanwhile I just so happened to check the time. It's two thirty in the morning, an hour past the time I was supposed to be calling Jackie. So while BB was still in the bathroom, I shot Jackie a text. "Hey beautiful, you still up?". I wrote. About five minutes past and I'm standing there thinking to myself like damn, I hope I didn't fuck up. Then a text came across my screen. "Luckily for you I am. I just got out of the tub. What are you still doing up Mr.?" she wrote. I quickly responded back...

"Well I just left my boys house. I had some business to handle. I apologize for hitting your line so late." I wrote back. I know what you're thinking and no I didn't lie. I just didn't tell the whole truth. She responded back...

"Nah, your fine. So should I still be looking forward to that phone call, or no?" she asked. Before I could respond BB had returned to the kitchen and started kissing and sucking on my neck with nothing on rubbing all over me as if she was ready for round two or something. All I know is I got to get rid of BB so I can be able to call Jackie, but how? Bingo, I got it. I made a very weird look fall upon my face. A look that I have practiced a million times to perfection causing her to take a step back...

"What's wrong L.A." she asked. A confused look fell upon her face...

"Baby girl get dressed, I need to drop you off at Bossman's house. My OG just texted me to meet her at the hospital." I said worriedly. The palms of her hands quickly cupped my chin...

"Oh my god is she okay?" she asked with concern. As our eyes locked, I force a tear to run down the corner of my eye to seal the deal...

"I'm really not sure what's going on sweetheart." I said convincingly.

"Okay honey I understand. let's go." she said. She put on her bra, panties and dress while I texted Jackie and said...

"Yes, please give me twenty minutes. I'm driving home now." I said. By the time BB and I made it to the car Jackie had responded...

"Okay, twenty minutes and THAT'S IT!" she texted back. BB and I got into the car and for that whole ride she was just all up on me...

"Why do they call you L.A.? If you don't mind me asking." she said. Taking a quick glance at BB...

"Well it stands for Lyrical Angel." I answered. She chuckles before responding...

" Well if you ask me, it should stand for Love Angel because what just happened about twenty minutes ago was pure heaven.", she passed before going on to say as she ran her fingers through my hair " I've never came so many times in my life before." she said. I glanced at her again with a smile on my face...

" I just have a way of paying attention to a woman's body." I said with confidence...

" Boy yes, you sure do...and how did you learn how to do those tricks with your tongue?" she asked. She rubbed her soft index finger across my bottom lip...

"Years and years of practicing how to tie the stem of a cherry into a bow with my tongue and eating pudding cups without a spoon." I answered...

"Well that practice paid off." she said.

"Thanks." I said. I pulled out my phone and called Bossman and all I could hear in the background was Chrystal screaming and moaning...

"Hel....hello?" Bossman said out of breath sounding as if he wasn't skipping ah beat...

"A..ah... Bossman, dude I need to drop BB off at ya crib. I got an emergency." I said. that was Bossman and mines code. Whenever either one of us say the phrase " I got an emergency" it means I got another chick I gotta get to ASAP...

"Alright L.A., the door is open" he quickly replied...

"Cool, I'm pulling up now. ONE." I said.

"One." he responded. I pulled up into the driveway...

"Alright baby girl... give me your number and I'll call you." I said which I didn't end up doing, but at the time it sounded like the right thing to say. She gives me her number and leans in to give me a kiss, ending the kiss biting my bottom lip...

"That was amazing. Call me so we can do it again sometime" she said.

"I got you baby girl." I said as I watched her as she made it into Bossman house safely. Then I pulled off. I glance at the clock on the radio. It's two forty-five am. I call Jackie. She answered the phone in such a soft seductive tone, I almost melted when she said...

"Hello...I see you do know how to be on time." Jackie said... I chuckle offering a quick response...

"Actually Mrs. Lady I am five minutes early." I said. with a hint of sarcasm in her voice...

"Oh your right, my watch must just be an hour and fifteen minutes early." she said. I can tell that she is feeling some type of way about me not calling when I said I would, so I apologized...

"Jackie, I apologize I truly do. I don't want you to think that I'm like these other brothers that can't stick to their word, I'm not." I said. Silence filled the phone before she responded...

"Tell me something I didn't already know." she said in a "matter of fact" tone. "L.A. if I thought you were like these other knuckle heads I would have never given you the time of day." she said. I pulled up

to my house, went inside and lay across the couch to continue our Congo...

"But as I can recall it correctly earlier this evening you blew me off when I first tried to talk to you." I said...

"I did... didn't I." she said sounding almost unsure of her actions...

"Yeah, you did. What was up with that?" I asked. She was quiet for a moment before finally offering a reason...

"To be honest with you L.A., when a brother sees me all he sees is "Eye Candy". A Carmel toned, five-foot three woman with a phat ass and a nice rack. Therefore they get no play... and I thought you was one of those brothers. Until you came correct." she said.

"So you're saying I'm different? I asked. I detected a slight grin on her face as she responded.

"If I didn't think so...trust me you wouldn't have even made it this far." she said matter of fact.

"True...true." I said.

"So Mr. L.A. what exactly is it that you do for a living, if you don't mind me asking." she asked. Something's telling me that she already knows I'm into the drug game, so not to scare her off or sound typical, I just told her what my second occupation was...

"Well, I'm a wedding singer." I said...

"Oh really...how long have you been doing that?" she asked.

"Doing what? Weddings? Or singing period?" I responded with a question of my own.

"Both." she said.

"Well I have been singing since about the fifth grade doing talent shows and what not. Then about three years ago I transitioned into doing weddings. My cousin paid me to sing at her wedding and a friend of hers that was engaged was there. She liked what she heard so she booked me, after that my voice became my occupation." I said. My legal one anyways.

"That's what's up. You gonna sing for me?" she questioned.

"When? Tonight?" I asked.

"Yes please...I mean unless you scared or something." she said playfully.

"Never scared my baby, but what exactly do I get in return?" I asked.

"Umm...what would you like?" She asked. Asking that question was like asking a kid in the candy store "do you want candy?".

"How about a wish?" I asked.

"Well even though I'm not a genie that sounds fair." she said eagerly awaiting to hear my voice.

I started singing "Signs of Lovemaking" by Tyrese. Why? Well for one I like the song. Two, I'm a Capricorn so it starts off so perfect, and three, I know hitting these notes are about to have her wet as shit... I finished singing and silence filled the air...

"Hello?" I said softly. Sounding as if her life had been changed, she offered a response...

"Oh my god, you have such a beautiful voice—", pausing to clear her throat she continued, "You make the words sound so sexy." she said softly.

"Thank you love." I said. Now it's time for me to use my one wish, and I have the perfect idea...

"Why did you pick that song?" she asked.

"Well, I have my reasons. I figured you would like it though" I replied.

"I did...So I guess I owe you a wish now." she said.

"Yes, actually I think you do. And I wish to play unlimited Truth or Dare." I suggested. She let out a little chuckle...

"Really? So what are the rules to this?" she asked. See my voice is a weapon. Sometimes I use it for good and sometimes for evil, I think tonight will be one of those nights where I use it for something that's so evil it feels good...

"Well its basically truth or dare, the only difference is that ANYTHING goes." I explained. Sounding a bit excited...

"Okay, I think I might like this. You start." she said. See the trick to this game is to ease your way into the convo that you really want to have. Watch and learn...

"Okay, Truth or Dare?" I asked.

"Truth." she replied.

"Is it true that you think I'm a good kisser?" I asked.

"Yes, you are a very good kisser actually. My turn. Truth or Dare?" she asked.

"Truth." I countered.

"Is it true that since you're a Capricorn that you are a freak?" she asked. I sensed a smile on her face as she asked the question.

"Now I wouldn't say a freak, more like a demon or Love Angel." I answered.

"Oh, so that's why they call you L.A.." she said. I can tell by her voice that she's smiling...

"No, I told you why they call me L.A., but if that is the reason why you want to call me L.A. then I'm fine with that. But any who, Truth or Dare?" I said. Now if she picks dare it let's me know two things. One, she is open to new things, and two, she might have a little freak in her as well...

"Uh...let's go with Dare." she said. BINGO! I relaxed my tone...

"I dare you to take off everything you have on and lay across your bed." I dared. Silence filled the line for a moment...

"Ummm...you are going to have to think of another dare...because when you called I was already laying down with nothing on. So your late Mr." she said. So I'm just lying down thinking to myself, damn, it seems like she's ready...

"Okay...then I dare you to close your eyes and listen to the sound of my voice. Picture everything that I'm saying and gently massage your clit.... Can you do that for me?" I asked in a very deep tone. I was shocked when she replied in the softest sexiest voice.

"Yes Papi." she answered

"Picture me pulling up to ya house and you hear a knock at the door. You see me and open the door, and as I step in, I close the door and ram you back into the wall. I start kissing you all over your neck while playing with your pussy." I hear her begin to let out a moan, so I knew she was understanding the assignment, so I continued." I pick you up and wrap your legs around my waist. You begin pulling my hair while I'm sinking my teeth into your neck. I carry you into the kitchen and lay you across the counter. I slowly start pealing your clothes off with my teeth Once I strip you down to your purple thong I walk over to the freezer and grab a cube of ice. I make my way back over to you putting the ice cube in my mouth and start running it all over your neck slowly working my way down to your chest. I start running the ice down your stomach, and the closer I get to your warm pussy the wetter you are getting, and the quicker the ice begins to dissolve in my mouth. I prop your legs up on my shouldered and I sit what was is left of the ice cube on your clit as I softly kiss the lips of your pussy." She let's out another moan of satisfaction, so I continue..."I take my long, thick tongue and slowly run it up and down dividing the lips of your pussy, running circles around your clit." I hear another moan get let out so, so far I can tell she likes receiving oral pleasure...and that's just awesome cause I like giving it. As I pause to listen to her sexy settle moans I hear her whisper into the phone...

"Ah...put it inside me...I'm about to cum." So I continued with my story allowing her to reach Maximum levels pleasure from it...

"I come up and slap my dick up against the lips of your pussy. Before I ease myself inside of you." I then hear her damn near scream through the phone as she reaches her climax. After giving her a moment to recuperate I then offered a response... "I see you enjoyed my story." I said. Slightly out of breath she offered a reply.

"Mmmm...yes, yes I did. It was very vivid. I could almost picture myself there." she said.

"Well truth be told Mrs. Jackie if you were here or I there, trust me, the events would have continued." I said.

"Is that right?" she asked. She offered the question as more of a statement.

"Yeah...that's right—-" pausing to analyze the sound of her voice before continuing, "It sounds like you ready to fall asleep now." I said. She replied in such a mellow voice, damn near a whisper...

"Actually I am." she replied. She started laughing...

"Oh I see you tap out quick." I said in a teasing way.

"Nah, Nah, Nah... don't get it twisted, if you were here, you would tap out before I would...But since you not I'm sleepy." she said.

"Well for one I wouldn't tap out, and two, who's fault is it that I'm not there?" I said. A brief moment of silence danced through the phone before she replied...

"That would be my fault, but I'm a lady before anything." she said...

"And I respect that, that's why I like you." I said. Responding as if she was truly shocked...

"Oh you like me huh?...Good...I like you too." she said...

"Well I'm glad we are both on the same page." I said. My phone began to beep letting me know that I have an incoming call coming through. I looked down at my phone...its Duce...

"Hold on baby girl I gotta put you on hold for a second." I said. Sounding a little irritated she responded...

"Okay, even though its ten after four in the morning." she said...

"I know and I am sorry. Hold on really quick." I said...

"K." she replied sounding baffled. I clicked over...

"Hello..." I answered.

"Yeah, L.A, you and Bossman meet me at Casper's spot in thirty minutes." Duce ordered.

"Alright." I responded. He hung up and I clicked back over.

"Hello....Jackie?" I said.

"Yeah. It took you long enough." Jackie replied...

"My bad, that was my boss." I said...
"Calling you this late?" she asked.
"Yeah, I have to take care of something, so I gotta go." I said...
"...mmmm...okay L.A.." she said.
"As a matter of fact, what are your plans for this Friday?" I asked. Not even completely sure if I was free myself. She responded...
"Nothing, why?". she asked...
"I would like to take you out to dinner if you don't mind." I said. You could hear a staple drop on the floor with how quiet it got after the question...
"Sounds like a date. I'll send you my address." she said...
"Alright cool, I'll holla at you later, and I'll see you Friday." I said. We hung up and I could tell by the sound of her voice she really didn't want to hang up, but at that time it was Money over Everything...

K.I.M

(Keep In Mind)

Most people look for love in all the wrong places. Then they ultimately create this false perception of what they believe love to be. Everyone has a different opinion on what love means to them, and most of the time their mindset on love is set prematurely based on past events or problems in their lives. Even though we do it its not good to base the next relationship on what the last person did. But as humans we use that pain, that hurt, that distrust as an excuse not to love, or allow ourselves to be properly loved. True, you have the option to live "Young, Wild, and Free", but are you living so "Young, Wild, And Free" that you fail to realize that the love that you have been searching for is right in front of you.

*As Humans we Often put off or Neglect

our Emotions So They often cause the flow of love to stop or Yield, not allowing any passage...Don't.*....Honesty.

Friday

Its getting late and I have yet to hear anything from Jackie. Our

reservations are at ten thirty tonight and it's twenty after eight now.

Then my phone rings...

"Hello?" I answered.
"Hey L.A... Listen, I am so so sorry. I've been so busy this week I forgot to call you and let you know I wasn't going to be able to make it this evening." Jackie said. A slightly disappointed spirit fell upon me...
"Nah, its coo, Maybe another time." I offered.
"I promise I'll make it up to you. if I didn't have this emergency, I would have loved to be with you tonight." she said. Those painful words kept digging deeper into my heart. Then I reminded myself why I don't allow my emotions to take over...
"Nah, its cool love, maybe another time." I said. I hung up and called to canceled my reservations. I flop down on my couch. Damn, its Friday, I canceled all of my plans, now what am I going to do? "Lisa" I thought to myself. I pick up my phone and called Lisa's house number. Her soft
voice echoed through the phone...
"Hello?" Lisa answered.
"Hey beautiful, what's going on?" I asked.
"Hey L.A., nothing much, just got out of the shower." she said...
"Oh, I'm sorry did I interrupt you? Are you heading out?" I asked.

"Nah, I. not going anywhere. I don't have any plans for tonight. I have to be at work at three in the morning." she replied.

"Well if you don't have any plans maybe we could go out?" I asked her...

"That doesn't sound like a bad idea. What did you have in mind." Lisa asked. I just cancelled dinner reservations, its too late for a movie.... Ah...

"Do you bowl?" I asked. I love going bowling, with or without people, it's my second-best stress reliever...

"The questions is do you bowl well enough, NOT to get your ass whooped?" she said laughing with confidence...

"Oh it's on. Put on something nice for me. I'll be outside in thirty minutes." I said. Laughing as she spoke words of war...

"Will do loser." she said. I go and get dressed. I grab my gloves, towel, shoes, and ball on my way out the door. when I open the door there she is just standing there in a sun kiss red sundress. it was long enough for bowling and just tight enough to possibly throw me off my game...

"You look beautiful." I said...

"Thanks, you don't look too bad yourself loser." she responded. Laughing out loud at the shameful comment. I grabbed her bowling ball bag off the porch and placed them in the truck then escorting Lisa to the passenger seat. The ride to the bowling alley Lisa had a few questions for me. Good thing the ride was a short one...

"This was kinda out of the blue. What made you ask me to go out with you tonight?" she asked...

"Well to keep it one hundred with you I been had a thing for you. I just didn't know how to approach you. you are a very attractive and smart woman. I guess I was just afraid of rejection."

I said. A grin met the corners of her mouth...

"I'm gold to finally know that I wasn't the only on of us that felt that way." she replied. Our eyes meet and we both smile. moments later we pull up to the bowling alley...

"L.A. man, what's going on?" the clerk said. That's Polo, the owner of the bowling alley, and a borderline crack head. I met him a few years ago when I first started coming here. As soon as he found out who I was and what I do we created this mutual understanding and we came to

agreement. The agreement was that I dont pay for anything, food, drinks, etc....and there was no limit on it. And on every fifth visit I would hook him up with three eight-balls. He's so happy to see me, because today it just happens to be my fifth visit...

"Nothing much Polo baby, how's business? I asked.

"Good, good as usual...and who is this beautiful young lady? Polo inquired.

"Polo, this is a very good friend of mine Lisa. Lisa, this is Polo." I said. They both reached out for each others hand...

"Its nice to meet you Polo." Lisa said. He takes Lisas hand and brings the back of her hand to his lips...

"No Lisa, the pleasure is all mine, and may I say you look very beautiful." Polo said...

"Thank you ." she said. Polo, snapping back to reality and turning his attention to me...

"I got your lane already for you. Shall I have your regular sent over?" Polo asked. I looked over at Lisa...

"What do you drink sweety? I asked Lisa...

"Well seeing as though I have to go to work at three tonight nothing heavy." Lisa said. I turn my attention back to Polo, who just seemed to be mesmerized by Lisa's beauty. I don't blame him though...

"Uh, Polo...by any chance do you have any Arbor Mist...Tropical?" I asked...

"Nah, I don't think so, but I'll have my son shoot down the street to the liqueur store and grab some." Polo said...

"Good, send two bottles of that over with wings and fries." I told him...

"Will do." Polo said. I can tell by the way Lisa was looking are me as we walked over to "my lane" that she was feeling my boss-like mentality...

"So you come here a lot I see." she said smiling at me while I helped her with her shoes...

"Yeah, I like it here. it helps me relieve a lot of stress." I said. She then spoke with a puzzled look on her face...

"So you brought me out because your stressed?" she asked...Interrupted by an approaching voice...

"L.A. sweetheart, good to see you." a female voice called out. I know that voice from anywhere.

That's KeKe the bartender, one of the older ones anyway. I think mid-fifties. She's always trying to get me drunk and take me home. She's cute for her age, just not my type. And I'm not even sure those are her real teeth. I turned around to see her holding a tray with three shots of vodka which is my regular and two glasses of Arbor Mist...

"KeKe , hey how are you?" I asked. She sat the tray down before answering...

"I'm fine baby cakes—" reaching out for a hug as she continued "how are you?" she asked. Accepting her hug, I then felt her hand slightly grab and pinch my ass following up with a kiss on my cheek. I felt so nauseated...

"I'm good." I answered. Turning my attention to Lisa. " KeKe, this is Lisa. Lisa, this is KeKe." I said. Both women had this look in their eyes that could cut through a brick...

"Hello." they replied to each other dryly. Then KeKe turned her attention back to me...

"Well honey I just came over to bring you your drinks, and you know if.." she started to say when I cut in...

"Yes I know. If I need anything just hit my button." I said. She gave Lisa another devilish glance before winking at me and walking away...

"Um, am I missing something?" Lisa asked confused. Placing a hand on her cheek I responded in a soft tone...

"No sweety your not missing anything. and to answer your other question, no I'm not stressed and that's not the reason I asked you out tonight." I said...

"Well why then?" she mumbled. Well the truth of the matter was that my date with Jackie got canceled, so going out with Lisa was...just a rebound. But that's not what she wants to hear...

"Well to be honest, I was a little confused the other night when you kissed me on my neck, and I wanted to hopefully clear up the confusion" I said. I watched as she walked away to roll her pink and blue ball down the lane. With each moment I grew more and more attracted to her wanting to explore her insides...

"There should be no confusion. But if I didn't make my point clear enough—-" she said as she walked back over to the seat I was sitting in. Standing over me she leaned down cupping the tip of my chin with her fingers following up with a warm and passionate kiss. Slowly breaking her lips away from mine she said in a soft tone " Was that message clear?" she asked. A warm tingle shot through my legs as I stood up...

"Crystal. Oh, and good shot by the way" I said walking toward the lane to throw my ball, hitting a strike..."But not good enough." I said. Our food comes over to the table and we start to enjoying a few laughs while eating and throwing back shots of vodka and sipping on the wine. The night started to get late yet we're still enjoying ourselves to the fullest. I glanced at my watch and its twelve thirty am. While Lisa goes up for her next shot I shot Jackie a text, "Hey, you still busy huh?". I feel Lisa's hands running through my hair. I look up...

"Hey, who you texting?" she asked. And even though she had a smile on her face I knew she was seriously curious...

"Uh, I'm just checking on my OG. She had to work tonight, I was just making sure she didn't need anything." I answered."

"Awww...isn't that sweet of you. It's your turn." she replied. Dodged a bullet on that one. I went up for my second shot and my phone vibrates. I check it...

" Yeah...unfortunately, I tried to get away early but I can't. I'm sorry." Jackie's text said. So I responded back...

"It's cool, hit me up when you get home." I texted back. After that I put my phone up and focus on my shot. BOOYA! I got another strike which put me in the lead with 218 to 203 in the sixth frame. I hear her sarcastically clapping in the background...

"Good job loser. But anyways, is she okay?" she asked. A slight crown came across my face...

"She who?" I asked confused.

" Your mother silly, I saw you texting before you hit that-" she held up quotations as shecontinued "Aaaamazzzing shot." she said sarcastically. Ignoring her hatting comment...

"Oh, she's fine." I said. As I turn around to grab my glass I hear a deep subtle voice fallout...

"Excuse me." I look to my left at the lane next to me. It's a guy about five foot seven, maybe a buck forty and possibly in his early twenties, dark complected and seemed to be well in shape.

We made eye contact and he offered his hand. "I see you got a pretty good arm on you." The man said...

"Thanks, I do what I can...and you are?" I asked...

"Damn where are my manners. My name is Marcel, but my friends call me Cell." he said. Pulling Lisa over to my side...

"What's up. I'm L.A. and this beautiful Angel is Lisa." I said. She waved without saying a word...

"Nice to meet you both, I apologize for being so straight forward, but it seems my date is running a little late. I don't want to start without her, yet I'm lacking entertainment, which leads me go my question. Are you a betting man L.A.?" he asked. I know his type. He's a professional scam artist. I know one when I see one...

"Depends on what I'm betting on, and if the price is right." I said. He reaches into his duffle bag where his ball was at and pulled out a stack of one hundred dlar bills. Pealing off a few...

"Well, I have three hundred dolla's say you don't hit eight or more pins this next roll." he said. This is how you play a con artist...

"I'm tempted to take you up on your offer, but nah, I'm good." I said. I turned back around to finish my game...

"Twelve hundred dollars!" he said enthusiastically. See, I get myself a sweety, someone willing to donate their money to the " me" foundation...

"One shot?" I asked. Nodding his head. "Double for a strike right?" I asked. He nodded his head in acceptance to the deal. So we shook hands on the bet. I felt a little bad taking his money so easily, but hey, that's life, you win some you lose some, but you live to fight another fight. I go to line up my shot, and as I take my last breath, I hear a soft voice whisper in my ear...

"If you make this meet me in the ladies room for your prize." Lisa said seductively. She slowly ran her lips across my ear, "and even if you don't make it, you can still meet me in the ladies room for your punishment." she said. I feel her hand slide something down in my front right pocket. I go to pull it out and stop short when I see and feel the silky red fabric. She smiles as she takes a few steps back when I turned to look at her biting her bottom lip. I'm thinking to myself as I'm realigning my shot, damn I get a chance to take his money and fuck Lisa. The overwhelming satisfaction of my two favorite pleasures being combined brought a big smile to my face and gave me an extra kick of confidence. I go to release the ball right along the gutter line *and made sure I put enough curve on it to make a hook shot. Rolling down the lane the ball*

hooked in exactly where I wanted it to, striking the pins at a well enough speed to knock them all down. "Twenty-four hundred easy." I said silently to myself. I turned around to see two things that had my adrenaline rushing, Lisa slowly walking down the walkway making her wag to the restroom, and Cell counting out my money. Inside I'm happier than a fat kid a Tim Horton's on

"Buy one get Five free" Fridays...

"Twenty one, twenty two, twenty three, twenty four hundred. Good shot L.A., I guess my odds where a little off." he said. Reaching out to give me my winnings I pulled off four hundred of the twenty four hundred and gave it back to him...

"Better luck next time. But excuse me ." I said. I made my down the walkway to the ladies room unseen. when j walked in I saw Lisa's red heels on the other side of the handicap stall...

"L.A. is that you?" Lisa called out. Without responding I walked into the handicap stall and locked the door behind me...

"I see you were determined to make that shot." she said as she walked up to me pushing me up against the wall. Watching as she slowly worked her way down to her knees, she unzipped my pants as I found my voice to speak...

"Yeah, what can I say you..." pausing as I watch her pull my dick out and softly kiss the tip of it, "you...you put an amazing offer on the table." I said. She started smiling when she looked up and saw me watching her. She slowly eased every inch of my dick into her throat struggling to breath and not choke while she plays with her own pussy. I'm not sure which one was dripping more all over the floor, her pussy or her mouth. I look down and softly cup her chin pulling her up to eye level and slowly turned her around. when I gripped the sides of her waist she slowly bent over pulling up her dress. She placed her hands on the wall as I smacked her on her ass. She let out a subtle moan

when I took the tip of my dick and slowly rubbed it against her wet pussy. Carefully dividing the lips of her pussy I eased inside of her. We both let out a moan of pleasant relief. The deeper I got into her treasure, the more grip she started to lose on the wall. I pushed her closer to the wall and pulled her closer to my body. Now we are chest to back, pelvis to ass and my hand wrapped around the front of her throat while I'm playing with her pussy with the other. the strokes from such a close distance continue to get deeper, and the deeper they got the harder they got and the tighter my grip becomes around her soft neck. I feel her begin to shake as she nuts all over my dick. I can tell she's losing her balance and I don't want her to tap out just yet. I slowly pullout, watching as her warm, creamy nut fell to the floor. I wrap her hair around my hand and turn her to me. I pick her up and ram her back into the door and the wall as she slowly eased my dick inside of her. She wrapped her legs round me tight like a boa constrictor snake wrapping itself around its prey to suffocate it as she started kissing and sucking all on my neck. The deeper I feel her nails digging into my back and the louder I'm making her moan is only helping my adrenaline rush. The possibility of us getting caught is scary, but its so scary that it makes me want to do it and it makes the experience ten times better. I loop my arms through hers acing my hands on her shoulders as I brought her closer to my bottom half digging deeper into her stomach. She sunk her teeth into my shoulder trying her hardest not to scream as she nutted all over my dick. The force of her soft and tender thighs wrapped around my waist and her pussy muscles constantly tightening up squeezing the life out of my dick. I fought the sensation of wanting to bust all off inside of her trembling walls and I pulled out. It was like she already knew I was ready to cum because as soon as I slid out of her she dropped to her knees begging to enjoy the rich flavors of my nut. So I fulfilled her wishes. She swallowed all of it, slowly gasping for air as she eased my dick out of her throat, softly rubbing it back and forth across her juicy, tender lips. As she slowly came to an upright position, placing her index finger on her bottom lip, gazing into my eyes..

"Mmmm...that tasted better than I anticipated—" she stepped in closer, placing her hand on my chest as she continued, "Did you enjoy yourself? she asked. I nodded my head yes, it was more convenient. I could barely find my wind, let alone find words to go along with it. "Good, I enjoyed myself too actually. It seems like I enjoyed myself multiple times." she said as a grin fell upon her face. We both looked at each other as we heard the door open. I hoped on top of the toilet so that there was only one set of legs that could be seen. Lisa put her hands over her mouth trying not to laugh as the stranger announced herself...

"Hello...are you okay in there?" a female voiced asked. Clearing her throat, Lisa finally responded to the woman...

"Ye...yes, I'm fine, I just cramping..." Lisa said. She looked over at me.." I was just having a hard time getting something so big inside of me." Lisa said. She winked at me. Then we heard some shuffling...

"Here sweetheart, this should be a small enough size." the woman said. The woman's hand reached under the door to hand Lisa a tampon...

"Thank you so much." Lisa said while snickering...

"No, your welcome sweetheart. I hope you feel better." the woman said as she left the restroom. Both Lisa and I busted out laughing as Lisa threw the tampon at me...

"Oh my God...we almost got caught." she said with a hint of excitement in her voice. I stepped down off of the toilet moving in closer to Lisa like a lion stalking its prey, slowly leaning in for a kiss I whispered...

"And that rush that your feeling is the best part." I said. We shared another warm kiss before fixing ourselves. I was the first to leave. "I'll meet you out there. Make sure you fix your hair." I said. She smiled as I walked out of the door and over to the bar unseen...

"Hey KeKe sweetheart, send Rhaychel over with two more glasses of wine." I said. She looked at me with a sense of longing, followed by a quick response...

"I sure will honey." She leaned in and gracefully placed her hand on top of mine as she continued. "L.A. you know you don't have to pretend your not interested in me." she said. Pretending, I thought to myself? No, the vibe she was getting was that of an accurate one. Not really knowing how to let her down smooth, I was just truthful with her...

"KeKe listen, you are a very beautiful unique woman, and still relatively young any man would be lucky to have you...but your not my type, and I truly apologize if I led you to believe otherwise." I said. She said not a word. She was speechless. The look on her face was full of disappointment, and embarrassment. I could feel her eyes following me as I walked away. By the time I got back to my lane Lisa was already there sipping on the last of her glass of wine...

"That guy...ummm....Cell?" Lisa said...

"Yeah, what about him?" asked. He couldn't have gone far, he left his jacket...

"He was looking for you. He said that he would be right back, his date was pulling up and he went to meet her" she said gesturing her hands toward the alley lane before continuing. " But it is your turn Mr." she chided. Laughing at the score and teasing Lisa for having lost the game, I grabbed my ball and took my mark, lining up my shot to the T...

"Oh there he is!" a voice called out. I turned around and to my surprise there she was, standing there in a dark blue sundress with colorful leggings on. When her eyes met mine she froze..."Honey this is the man I was just telling you about that just won a nice sum of money from me bowling... Baby, this is L.A., L.A. this is my lady—-" Cell was in the middle of saying but cut off by my immediate response to the introduction...

"Jackie." I said. A puzzled look fell upon Cells face...

"You two...know each other?" Cell asked curiously. Jackie tried to speak but quickly came to silence when she heard the tone in my voice as I spoke with words that could have cut right through her...

"Apparently not...so this was your emergency?" I asked Jackie. Cell had a bewildered look on his face as his focus shifted to Jackie. Jackie didn't have a chance to answer my question before Cell offered a question of his own...

"What is he talking about...emergency... And who is he to you?" Cell asked Lisa. I could see the fear in her eyes grow deep as she spoke...

"H..he..he's just...-" Jackie hesitated. I interrupted allowing the problem hopefully be resolved...

"I'm nobody, Jackie and I are just good friends, nothing more, trust me, and as far as the emergency, we talked earlier, and she wanted my opinion on what to get her boyfriend as a "Just Because Gift" and she was suppose to be getting back at me about some ideas, but she said an emergency came up." I said. It seemed that the explanation relaxed Cell and reassured his stable position with Jackie. I could tell that Jackie was shocked by how relatively quick I was able to come up with that on the spot. But looking past her light amusement I saw the look of shattered dreams of "what could have been" being blown away with every word I spoke. By this time Lisa had stepped away making her way to the counter to return her shoes...

"I'll meet you in the car honey." I said to Lisa. Cell then turned his attention to Jackie as I continued speaking..."Yeah Cell man, you have a very special woman here on your hands...Its not everyday you find someone so loyal, honest, and loving to her man.." I said as I paused to glance at my watch and its already ten after two in the morning, and Lisa works at the hospital not far from here. I'll just take her I thought to myself before continuing.. "But I do have to go, Lisa has to be at work at three am, but it was nice to finally meet you Cell, and

I'm glad that I ran into you tonight Jackie." I said sincerely. Cell and I shook hands as he spoke...

"It was nice meeting you as well. Maybe we could do this again sometime, you know, give me a chance to win my money back." Cell said. He smiled as I nodded my head to his offer...

"Sure I don't see any harm in that, as a matter of fact.." I paused. I saw KeKe coming down the walkway delivering the tray with the wine herself.." Drinks are on me tonight. Its Arbor Mist Tropical." I finished. Cell accepting the two glasses with a shocked look on his face...

"Honey.... this...this is your favorite isn't it?" he asked Jackie. Not wanting to speak she placed the rim of the glass to her soft lips just nodding her head in acknowledgement to his question.

My response was well in tuned with his facial expression. Acting clueless I offered some reassuring closer...

"Oh wow, I had no ides it was your favorite Jackie. I just like the smooth taste, my mother used to drink it and when she wasn't around I would sneak me a glass." I said. Once again that smooth and unpracticed comment seemed to have relaxed Cell and cleared up any tension in the air. We shared our last goodbyes and I made my way to the door, stopping at the corner office where I already knew I would find Polo. I dropped off his package and I made my way to the car. As I was walking to my car I couldn't help but think to myself, like damn, she got a man, she played me. Why didn't she just tell me rather than leading me on? The continuous questions rambling through my head quickly came to a halt when I saw Lisa sitting in my car, arms folded. When I got inside the car I asked..."Do you mind if I drop you off at work?.. Lisa said nothing. She just sat there in silence. So I spoke again a little bit louder this time..."Um...Hello...Lisa... would you like for me to drop you off at work? I asked again. Her silence was broken when she calmly spoke...

"No, you can drop me off at home—-" she said. She glanced over at me with hurt in her eyes as she continued..."She was one of your ex's wasn't she?" she asked. Hoping to clarify the situation I spoke with confidence...

"No, she was just someone I met at the lock-in party." I told her. The with quickness she offered another question...

"The one you brought home that night? she asked. A puzzled look fell upon my face before responding...

"Damn, you watching me or something?" I questioned. She folded her arms as she spoke...

"No. I saw your car was in your driveway and I wanted to come over and give you some company, only when I walked up to your porch to knock at the door I heard loud screaming and moaning coming from the kitchen. I figured you had enough company for one night so I went back home." she said. I wasn't even aware me and BB was even that loud that night, and now that I think about it I did have a few missed calls from Lisa that night as well...

"No, that was a different girl." I said. Lisa shook her head as we pulled up to her house. She got out and stood outside the car holding the door open...

"L.A., I had a very amazing time tonight, but I can to you that This, what we have between us, is just lust. L.A. you are going to make a special woman very happy one day, if you just open you heart and allow them in, but until then your just a nice smile, good dick, and intelligent. You truly a good guy. But you have so much potential to be great—-" she said as she leaned over the seat and gave me a kiss on my cheek..."I can see that, unfortunately I'm not that special woman... not for you anyways, but that's fine. I'll find my king one day...Prince Charming." she said. Even though I didn't want to admit it, but she was right. I did need to open up, but why, when my heart longed for someone I couldn't have. Someone that seemed forbidden to love. I waited as she walked away and made it into her house safely. I pulled

up a few houses and pulled into my driveway. I make my way into to house and hit the shower. I get out and get dressed. As I'm getting dressed I notice that I have a text message...

"I am truly sorry for what happened and not being honest with you about everything." Jackie wrote. True enough, Jackie was an amazing person, beautiful and smart, but life is too short to play second fiddle in a love triangle. When I didn't respond she posed a question..."Is it possible I can come over so we can talk?" she wrote. Talk! I looked at the clock and its after two thirty am

and the only things that are open after two thirty in the morning are strip clubs and legs. I already know how I am. If she comes over more then likely we are going to have sex. But see, I am not one to tear apart a happy home or relationship because in wouldn't want the same done to me. So I couldn't even put myself in that situation...

"Nah, you good. I understand, something's are meant to be kept secret. But no you can't come over, it's late and I'm really not in the mood for company—-. Jackie, I am going to be honest with you. I can't lie, I'm feeling you and I was hoping it could have been more, but I think it would be best if we just remained friends. Cell seems like a good guy and he seems to love you and you must love him. And I am not the type of man to break up a happy home." I texted back. Jackie understood where I was coming from, and after that night Jackie and I became the best of friends. There was always still that sexual tension there but we both respected each other enough to not allow our lust for each other to ruin our friendship. I do wonder how things would have worked out with Jackie, but some things happen for the best....and some doors are better left unopened...

K.I.M.

Love VS. Lust Mind. VS. Body
In the dictionary the word "Love" is defined as: To cherish, to feel a passion, devotion, or tenderness for... In other words love is a passion that touches your soul if its real...Have you ever loved someone so much that just hearing their voice made you feel at peace? Understand the we are not talking about a friendship love, I'm talking about a Soulmate love, that love where you feel so greatly about someone your face lights up when you hear their name. That love that hurts you to see them with someone else knowing you can give them more than what their heart desires. That love that gives you a frog in your throat trying to express your love to them, or that love that makes an impact on your life each day for the better, and helps you to become a better you. If a men of woman hasn't or can't make you feel that way then you have not yet encountered true love... You are stuck in a dark realm of Lust which is defined as: A intense or unveiled sexual desire, an intense longing...In other words the complete opposite. When you are lusting for someone you think that you are in love, when in reality there's nothing more then just a physical connection...Think back to a time when you thought you were in love, and come to find out the sex was just good, or you didn't feel the same way about that person after you have had sex...When you first meet a person you didn't say "Damn that's my soulmate." because there is always a physical attraction first. So you may have said" Damn, he look good" or "Damn she is sexy". As humans it natural to have a physical attraction to someone before an emotional attraction...But realize that there is a thin line between Lust and Interest... Within the first five minutes of meeting someone you can

tell if you have an interest in them potentially being your spouse, someone special, or you can tell if you just want to bump and grind...Now I'm not saying any things wrong with a little bump and grind, but a real woman or man holds to standards and respect for their temple.

Closer To My Dreams

(4 Years Later)
Phone Call
Its 8:30 am and my sleep has been broken by the sound of my phone ringing. I rolled over to answer my phone without checking the Caller ID...and a voice said...
"Hello?" By the foreign tone and the excitement in the voice I knew off rip who it was...
"Ace my man...what's going on." I said. Ace is my jeweler. We met about three years back when I came to his shop, and I fell in love with his work. He is an older guy, Chinese, mid fifties, and cool as hell and always hooking me up with custom details...
"L.A. baby...I got good news for you.." Ace said enthusiastically...
"What's up Ace?" He's always calling me with good deals on his limited and custom pieces...
"Ya watch just came in this morning...I just opened up the store, so you can come by and pick it up." he said. That was quick. I had jut bought a Frank Muler Watch from his shop about four days ago, but Ace said it would tame about two weeks to get it back because he had to send it out to get what I wanted done to it...
"Did you check it out?" I asked. His swift response to my question gave me peace of mind...
"Just as you wanted it. Black leather band with the letters L.A. stitched in the leather—" I quickly interrupted with a follow up question...
"What about my center Ace?" I asked. I wanted the original centerpiece removed and replaced with a platinum L.A. with

seventy-four D-colored, one carrot VVS-1 stones placed throughout the initials behind the glass...

"Yes...yes of course, I couldn't have done it better myself." he said. A grin fell upon my face as I spoke...

"Ace, man you know how to treat me good—" I said...

"Nonsense, when you come? he asked. Sitting up in the bed...

"I'll be there in an hour." I said...

"Okay see you then." he said before hanging up. He funny as hell. I got up, brushed my teeth and washed my face, then I hoped in the shower. I get out and throw on a gray Polo jogging fit with a pair of J's... I grab my keys, wallet, and cellphone off of my dresser and grabbed my briefcase from under my bed and headed out the door. I pull up to the mall. Its a nice day out. The sun is shining and sundresses are everywhere. I park my car, grab my briefcase and make my way to Aces shop...

"L.A.!" Ace said in excitement as his hands went up in the air as if he hasn't seen me in years. But that's nothing new, he's always happy to see me. I guess because he already knows that I don't care about price. If I want it I get it..."My friend...sit...sit.." he said. I took a seat in the chair next to one of the showcases while he finished up with a customer in the store. After about three

minutes he politely finished up with his customer, walked the man to and out the door , the locked the door behind him. Clapping his hands together with excitement..."Ah...my friend, please come, come follow me." he said waving his hands over to the back room door. I followed him into the backroom with my briefcase in hand. Once I crossed the threshold I saw the glass table that had an object on top of it with a silk cloth beneath the object. I step closer...

"Nice...its exactly how I pictured it, now we can get down to business." I said. Glowing with excitement the little Chinese man grabbed the watch and placed it inside of the original casing and put it inside a store bag...

"L.A...you...you good man, good customer, and you always handsomely tip—" he paused to pull out another box out of a drawer from the table..."For that loyalty I had this made for you." He said handing the box to me. I opened it up...

"Damn Ace.." A white gold premium Rolex with my initials in graved in the band. ."I don't know what to say...Ace man, thanks...So what's my damage? I asked. Shaking his head...

"No "thanks" needed my friend...and let's see—" he said as he put on his glasses that were hanging from around his neck and started flipping through his little black book..."Ah. Twenty eight thousand." I sat my briefcase on top of the glass and opened it...

"I thought it was a little more then that—" handing him two bricks of blue strips... "What you do, give me a discount? I asked. The little Chinese man laughed while taking the money...

"You take care of me L.A., I take care of you." he said. We shook hands . As he walked me to the front of the door of the tore and unlocked the door...

"It was a pleasure doing business with you my friend." I said patting his shoulder as I walked out of the door. I checked the time and its only 11:45 am, so I decided to grab me a bite to eat from the eatery. I went to go and stand in line at the little Coney Island they had in the mall...

"L.A...L.A. is that you?" a familiar voice called out. I know that voice ...No I couldn't be her. When I slowly turned around our eye met. She stood there glowing wearing a Michigan State T-shirt with a pair of yoga pants and J's on. Simple I know, but you don't understand, this woman can make a nuns uniform look absolutely stunning. She stood five foot five, caramel mocha toned, long hair, hazel eyes ,with soft lips and a smile that could brighten your day. Oh,

and did I mention she's very intelligent. My eyes must be playing tricks on me...

"Monique?" I said. Before I knew it I was feeling the warm embrace of her hugging me...

"Yes its me silly...Wow its been so long—" she said. Taking a step back to look at me..." Look at you." she said. She was right, it had been a long time since we have seen each other. Four years to be exact when she had her going away party for college...

"No, look at you Mrs. College girl. How have you been?" I asked her. We walked over to a table and sat down...

"I have been good. What about you? And how is your mom?" she asked. I've been missing you is what I wanted to say, but I held my tongue and simply just responded with...

"I'm pretty good actually and my mother is doing fine, thanks for asking. So what are you doing back?" I asked.

"Well actually I took this semester off to relax. I've been studying for four years straight, in deserve a break....You don't seem happy to see me." she asked a little hurt. Gazing into her beautiful brown hazel eyes it seemed as if every feeling and emotion that I had for her that I thought was gone came rushing back. Here I am sitting across the table from the woman I loved since just a youngster, and it was killing me not being able to tell her how I feel about her. I wanted to tell her so bad, but how would she have responded? I didn't want to ruin our friendship. But at the same time I don't want to miss out on the best thing that may have happened to me. But then again how would Bossman feel? He knows I'm a bit of a player, but this woman is something totally different...

"Nah, I am actually very happy to see you." I said...

"Mmmhmm...So what are you doing here by yourself with no girl on your hip little Romeo?" she asked teasingly. Trying my best to gather all my thoughts, I answered her question...

"Nah, no groupies today. I was just out stopping in to pick up a few things, plus in don't have anybody in my life special enough to get that Romeo treatment... well I do but...never mind. What about you, where are all your groupies? I said with a smile. She sat back in her seat as she spoke...

"I was actually on my way to Victoria Secrets. And I don't have any groupies. Everybody isn't blessed to have a voice like you." she said. I sat forward in my chair...

"And everybody isn't blessed to be as beautiful and as smart as you, and I didnt think that my voice impressed you.." I said. A slight grin fell upon her face as she spoke...

"Of course it did I just never bothered showing it. It seemed like you had enough applicants on your hands." she said. Applicants? What did she mean by that? Is she hitting on me?...

"Well maybe if someone worth my time, effort, and love would have put in an application it would have saved me a lot of time sorting through those applications" I said. Trying to change the subject she offered what surely would have been a question had she not been interrupted...

"So you still working—" she began...

"Dinner?" I asked quickly. She looked shocked by the interrupting outburst. I just couldn't hold it in any longer...

"What?" she asked surprised. I swallowed a little hard after seeing the arch of her eyebrow raise and it made me even more nervous to ask again, but this may be the one and only shot, and I had to take it...

"Would you like to have dinner with me?" I ask. My heart was damn near ready to burst out of my chest. A moment of silence filled the air before she finally spoke...

"Are you asking me to go out on a date with you?" she asked. And here comes the painful rejection, let's just throw the icing on the cake.

"I...I....ummm...I believe I am, yes.. "I fumbled out. My whole body seemed to have stiffened already anticipating her answer...

"Can I pick the place?" she asked. My eyes widened...

"What?" I asked. I leaned back in my chair in disbelief...

"Yes, I'll go out to dinner with you." she replied. A burst of relief flowed through my body. " What about Saturday... at 8:30?" I asked...

"Okay its a date. Here, take down my number." she said. I took my phone off my hip and handed it to her. She texted herself so that she'll have my number. I was still looking a bit confused, and I'm sure she could tell I was shocked by her response. "I'll make sure I bring my sum along with me Saturday." she said. We both shared a smile as we stood up. "Well—" she says as she steps over to me giving me a hug, "I gotta go. it was great seeing you. I'll text you my new address." she finished.

"It was great running into you as well...I'll see you Saturday" I said. We then parted ways. I stood in the middle of the mall watching her walk away toward Victoria Secrets and suddenly I get a text message...

"And don't worry, I won't tell my brother." she wrote. That made me feel not as bad. I watched as she disappeared down the hall. I couldn't it, I had the dumbest Cool-Aid smile ever. Leaving the mall after making a few more stops I had completely forgotten all about being hungry until I got back home. When I made it home I threw off my jacket, sat my bags on the kitchen table, washed my hands, and started to pulling something out to cook. While I am cooking, my house phone starts to ring. I answered...

"Sup." Bossman said...

"What's up Bossman, what's going on?" I asked...

"Shit really, L.A. man I can't call it. What you getting into tonight my baby?" he said. Bossman always seemed to find something to do on such a short notice...

"I don't ain't got nothing planned. Why what you got on the floor?" I asked...

"Shit I was thinking about sliding through this house party tonight." he said.

"Now you know Janel ain't letting your ass out the house to go to no damn house party." I said. Janel is Bossman woman. He tells me that they have been dating for a few months now. She's a very attractive woman, nice curves and she's smart with a good job...

"Ha, ha, funny. Actually she just left out for work. She has to work a double at the hospital tonight, so she ain't gotta know shit, you know how I do it." he said. Actually I know exactly how he does. See every time he steps into a relationship he starts off good, being faithful and everything. Then somewhere along the way I guess boredom kicks in. But I can't tell another man how to treat his woman...

"Alright man, what time?" I asked. Looking down at my watch as I made my plate. I figured I would do me some blueberry pancakes and eggs, something simple...

"9 o'clock..but umm...she got the car." he said...

"Of course she does. Alright man just make sure yo ass ready, I'll pick you up at 9:30." I said...

"Alright, One." he stated...

"One." I said before I hung up. He's always finding some reason to get out of the house. Good thing I just picked me up a new fit, a cherry red True Religion jean top and bottom with some fresh Air Forces to go with it while I was out at the mall. I sat down at the kitchen table getting ready to enjoy my meal when I hear a knock at the door. I wasn't expecting any company. A slight frown fell upon my face and then I thought about it, maybe its Monique. I have been living in the same house since she went off to college. A smile spread from ear to ear on my face as I walked up to the front door and opened it...

"Hey L.A..." Janel said. The smile on my face quickly dropped to the floor...

"Janel?...What are you doing here?" I asked. She made her way past me without offering and answer to my question. Bossman just said she went to work, but wait, how did she know where I lived? She

stepped into the middle of the hallway and turned around toward me...

"You don't look happy to see me." she said as she untied her tan trench coat unveiling what was underneath, which ended up being this short skin tight red dress. Immediately there was two things I can tell off rip.. One, she didn't have a bra on, I could see her nipple piercings protruding through the dress, and Two, she didn't have on any panties. That was a no brainer, she had them dangling from her fingertips. She dropped her coat to the floor. I'm just standing other stuck lost for words as she slowly pealed her dress off from her shoulders letting it drop to the floor. Her body seemed perfect, nice size everything, no stretch marks , no hair, no smell, and she had this cute little tattoo along her panty line that read "Slippery when Wet" with two droplets of water falling from one of the It's. She slowly walked over to me placing her hand on my chest as she slowly worked her way down to her knees...But for you to understand how we got to this spot, I have to take you back about three weeks ago...

K.I.M.

Karma is a BITCH

"What goes around comes around." Such a simple concept. It seems crazy that we would even need to discuss such a thing. The crazier part is that even though it is a simple concept it is still commonly misunderstood or overlooked. People that lie and cheat on their spouses are constantly tormented everyday by the same question. "Why can't I find a good man or woman? Why do I keep getting hurt?" Well let's recap. The last few spouses you had that were willing to love you, you either slept with their best friend, sibling, or a random person. Or maybe you were dishonest, playing them for your own selfish needs. And you really didn't think that would come back and bite you in the ass? You do unto others as you would want done unto you. its never too late to change your ways, if you want true love, but it is too late to back track and reignite the love that you mistreated in the past. "Well what about me? I have never cheated, lied, or

mistreated any of my spouses and I still get hurt." The sad and unfair truth of today's society is that there are more people in the world that are willing to play with your heart and use your tenderness for love as your weakness. But process of elimination helps you find that "needle in the haystack" that will cherish your heart like the gold that it is. Remember the more you speak love into your existence, the closer you get to unlocking the doors to that enchanted feeling of love...

The Cookout

A few weeks ago Cell and Jackie had a little cookout. They invited a few mutual friends, coworkers from their jobs , and of course family...basically everyone. They threw the cookout party to celebrate their anniversary. Yeah they ended up getting married two years ago, and me being a good friend of Jackie's she asked me to attend even though she knows I don't really care for Cell because of the way that he treats her. They have been married two years and they have two beautiful little children together, yet Cell still sleeps with other women, Jackie's sister

Tameka being one of them. I have tried to tell Jackie about Cell, but she's so in love with this boy that she's blind to the Red Flags, or maybe she's just ignoring them. Either way I hate watching as he pretends to be so madly in love with her when clearly his actions show otherwise. I pulled up in my black and gray Dodge F-150 and parked right in front of their house. I got out and walked toward the backyard. Bossman told me he was swinging through but I didn't see his car, so he must not be here yet. I make it to the backyard and I see Cell at the grill...

"Cell, what's up." I said. Looking over his shoulder as he was cleaning the grill...

"Nothing much L.A., you a little early man. But I'm gold you made it." he replied.

"Yeah well I only became because Jackie asked me to." I said. He knows I don't really care for him and I believe the feeling is mutual...

"Oh, well you know your always welcome." He responded with a hint of sarcasm in his voice.

"So I hear Bossman is supposed to be coming as well, him and his lady friend." he said. See, Cell and Bossman have grown closer ever since Bossman helped Cell start up his nonprofit organization, which is really just a cover up for drug housing and an easier way to clean up money. So I guess you could say they were good business partners...

"Yeah, that's what he told me." I said. I was kind of excited to finally meet Bossmans lady. See Bossman and I, we hang out and we used to pick up women together, but now he has a woman. I mean a real woman. She's so beautiful, and that body.. boy oh boy that body is so pleasingly cover that it sends chills down my body just looking at her. Now I have never seen her in person. Bossman has only showed me a few pictures. But today is the day that I finally get to meet this beautiful Goddess. A voice called out from behind me...

"Hey L.A.." the familiar voice said. I turned around...

"Hey Jackie—" reaching out to give her a hug then a kiss on the cheek I continued." you looking good as usual." I said. She had on this blue silk dress that came down a little above her knees with her legs glowing from the light of the sun...

"Thank you L.A, your looking good yourself. No groupies with you today?" she asked with a smile. Even after all this time she still gets a little jealous when I come around with another woman on my arm...

"Nah, no groupies. Just me today, but thank you." I said Our eyes were stuck on each other for a moment before getting rudely interrupted by Cell...

"Ah, L.A. you gonna help me get this meat on the grill?" Cell asked. I really didn't want to but Jackie gave me this look that spoke for itself without words...

"Yeah, sure I got chu." I said. A slight grin fell upon her face as Cell and we made our way through the back door to the kitchen grabbing the pans containing the hotdogs, ribs, and hamburgers. We make our way back to the grill when I hear the voice of an Angel. I turned to around to look only to see Bossman and his lady walking up the drive way speaking to Jackie. They made their way over to the grill...

"L.A. baby what's good...this is my lady Janel." Bossman said. I sat the pan I was holding down and grabbed her by her hand and kissed it...

"Its nice to finally meet you Janel. I have heard such good things about you." I said with a smile...

"The pleasure is all mine L.A.." she said. The smile she gave me had me on stuck, speechless. I watched as Bossman went around introducing Janel to everyone showing her off like a gold medal. When they returned to the table Bossman and I excused ourselves. Leaving the ladies to talk amongst themselves while we walked over to the grill where Cell was...

"You got a cold little piece on your hands right there." Cell said to Bossman while flipping the hamburger patties on the grill...

"Yeah man she a cold piece, but I'm starting to get bored already." Bossman said. Cell let out a laugh...

"Bossman what chu mean bored? Y'all only been together what two maybe three weeks. You gotta learn patience man." Cell said. Bossman responded swiftly as if he was already anticipating Cell to say such a thing...

"Well it isn't that the pot calling the kettle black. How long have you Jackie been married? And how long have you been fucking her sister?" Bossman said to Cell. A moment of silence filled the air before he continued. "Exactly." Bossman said eagerly as if he was satisfied to have made his point. I stood there as the two went back and forth, quietly, trying not to be overheard by the ladies. The whole time I keep noticing that Janel is keeping her eyes on me, and I can't lie I'm feeling her. We shared another glance before I was interrupted by the pointless argument about which one of them was right and which one was wrong...

"Honestly, both of you are fucking stupid if you ask me." I said. They both paused and turned their attention to me, both looking surprised. "Cell you have a very beautiful, loving, honest, and intelligent woman that has given you two beautiful daughters and has been nothing but loyal to you and your fucking around with her sister behind her back.—" Turning my attention to Bossman..."And you...You have found a beautiful young lady that has so far been able to put up

with your ass, longer then any other chick has, and she could possibly be the best thing that has ever happened to you. You both have good, no, great women in your lives yet you still make the dumbass conscious decision to mistreat them." I said annoyed. Both Bossman and Cell looked at each other for a moment, then collectively gave out a bit of a chuckle...

"So when did you become Romeo?" Bossman said followed by a mocking quote from "Romeo and Juliet" by Cell...

"Romeo oh Romeo, where forth art thou Romeo?". Both Bossman and Cell begin to laugh...

"Yeah yeah yeah...Call it what you want. I just know when a woman should be treated like a queen, something y'all have clearly yet to comprehend...and you might not ever comprehend until its too late. When your woman has grown tired of your bullshit and pain your

causing, and she finds her worth and purpose as well as the strength to leave, then you'll then see their true value." I said. My words, followed by their laughter gave me a little more incentive for me to leave..."I'll be right back." I said. I walked into the house to go to the restroom. Before I could even make it through the kitchen I was ambushed by two beautiful little children. Wrapping themselves around my legs...

"Hey uncle Frank, hey uncle Frank!" they called out together...

"Now ladies what did we talk about?" I asked them both. Nisha and Ball quickly jumped to their feet...

"Sorry uncle L.A." both girls said together. I pulled out my wallet and gave them both fifth dollars...

"Now that's more like it." I said with a smile. The girls started jumping up and down excitedly...

"Thankyou!" Nisha and Bell said together. They both gave me a hug and a kiss and then ran off to go and play. I made my way up stairs to the restroom to take a leak. As I'm standing there in the restroom pissing...Janel walks right in...

"Whoa...someone's in here." I said. I see her eyes catch a glimpsy at my dick and she bites her bottom lip...

"Oh, I'm sorry." she said as she closed the door. And I'm just thinking to myself...Damn did she just do that on purpose or by mistake?...anyways. I washed my hands and I opened the door and Janel is standing against the wall. She lifted her head up and our eyes meet, and before I knew it she stepped in a little closer. Then her lips touched mines. In the back of my mind I'm like "Damn her lips are so soft and warm its ridiculous", caught up in the moment I found myself softly caressing her cheek and neck...then I hoped back to reality, pushing her off of me...

"Janel...baby girl what are you doing?" I asked her. She took a step back leaning up against the wall...

"I'm sorry...I overheard you taking up for me. I thought you was feeling me." she said. Oh damn is it possible Jackie heard me as well?...

"Did anyone else hear me?" I asked...

"If you are referring to Jackie...no she didn't hear you." she said...

"Good." I said. A breeze if relief settled over me. Then I noticed that Janel had this sad look on her face of disappointment, or maybe a feeling of rejection...

"Janel...I ain't gonna lie to you baby girl, you are cold blooded." I said... She stepped closer into my personal bubble...

"You think so?" she said as she grabbed my hands and placed them on her ass before adding a second question..."So what do you think about this L.A.?" she asked. I was at a loss for words. Before I could even muster up a thought she grabbed my dick and started kissing me, and even though I didn't want to, I had to stop her...

"Janel baby...listen...you are my homeboy's woman, I cant—" I was saying before I was interrupted and silenced by the soft touch of her finger pressing up against my lips and she grabs my phone out of my pocket and calls herself...

"I like that your fighting what you really want to do to me, but I got something that might change your mind." she said. She really has no clue what I would do to her, but when she whispered that into my ear and ran her tongue across my neck...boooy I almost melted. She walked off and left me with my knees buckling. I pulled myself together and fixed my clothes. As I mad my way

down stairs back to the cookout I noticed that Bossman and Cell was still engaging in the same, pointless conversation as they were when I left. I quickly grew tired of being in their company. It was already getting late so I figured I would call it a night. I make my way over to Jackie and a

few other ladies and say my goodbyes. Leaning in for a hug...

"Alright Jackie, I had a good time. Thanks for inviting me but I believe its time for me to go." I said. She could tell that I really didn't enjoy myself. She offered a question in the form of a statement as she ended the hug with a soft kiss on my cheek...

"So you really have to leave L.A.? she asked. I could see the look of disappointment in her eyes as I nodded my head confirming her statement. "Well at least take you a plate to go." She offered...

"Okay love, I'll talk to you later. I'll have Cell fix it." I said while turning away and made my way towards the fellas. Cell, Bossman and myself made our way into the kitchen and engaged in a mutual conversation about this upcoming Sundays Lion's game while Cell fixed my to-go plate...

"I got season tickets for the lions games this year." Cell said...

"Aw man you wasting your time, and money. The damn Lions suck." Bossman called out in a joking manner, sparking up yet again another unnecessary debate. Meanwhile I feel my phone vibrate. Its a text message that reads...

"Hey L.A., its me Janel. Save my number." it said. I ain't thinking nothing of it so I respond back and say...

"Okay beautiful will do." I texted back. Now I probably shouldn't have called her beautiful, but there's no harm in a little flirting right? Wrong! While Cell, Bossman, and myself continue kicking it my phone starts to vibrate again. This time its a picture message from Janel. I am truly hesitant on opening it while Bossman is standing right here...but j did anyways. I damn near dropped my phone when the picture loaded and popped up. The boys saw me fumbling with my phone...

"Uh, you good L.A.? Cell asked...

"Yeah, I'm good...don't forget the Mac & Cheese." I said to him. He turned to open up the oven as I look at the picture again. Its a picture of her playing with her wet juicy pussy, and from the looks of it she's a creamer. And she has a nice little piercing. I felt a slight grin start to fall upon my face, and I just so happen to look behind me and Janel was walking into the kitchen. I see her bit her bottom lip. Its crazy how no one else caught that gesture she made. So I grabbed my plate and say my goodbyes...

"Alright y'all I'm out." I said nodding my head at Cell before giving Bossman some dap...

"Alright L.A. man I'll holla at you tomorrow?" Bossman asked...

"Yeah Bossman I gotchu." I replied. Janel then gives me this dirty seductive look and says...

"It was a big pleasure meeting you L.A.." she said. Reaching out for her hand as I responded...

"Nah, Janel the pleasure was all mine." I said. Bossman walked me out to my car...

"Hey, L.A....Duce wants to meet with us in three weeks." Bossman says. A bit stunned I said...

"About what?" I asked. Bossman shrugged his shoulders...

"I'm not sure man, I just know he wants to see us." he said. We made it to my car, gave each other some more rap before I hoped in the car and pulled off. I get home and hit the shower then laid down. While flicking through the channels on TV I doze off. The night is not over though. I know, I thought it was too until my phone started ringing and I'm laying there thinking to myself who the hell is this calling me at two in the morning? I roll over and grab my phone off the nightstand and answer it...

"Hello?" I answered. My posture straightened up after hearing a soft voice reply...

"Hey L.A." the female voice said. I looked down at my phone, and of course the number is not saved so I have no idea who this could be, but before I could respond the voice started again.

"So I assume by your silence you don't have my number saved." the voice said. I quickly went to check my messages...

"Actually I did save your number Janel. Its kinda late, what's up?" I asked. A brief moment of silence was left dangling in the air before she responded suddenly...

"Yeah I know, I just got out of the shower and I was laying down just thinking about that free show I got to see today." she said...

"Free show...what free show?" I asked. I knew I wasn't tripping. She did walk in on purpose...

"I saw you see me glance down when I walked in on you." she said. By this time I had sat straight up before responding...

"Nah, I didn't pay it any attention." I said with a hint of laughter in my voice...

"Yeah, okay well I was just calling to let you know, I like what I saw, and I'll be real with you I wouldn't mind test driving that." she said seductively. Truth be told after that comment I was stuck, just lost for words. Without giving me a chance to speak her soft set voice spoke again. "And don't worry, it will be out little secret. You can keep a secret can't you?" she asked. I already knew that her statement was referring to the whole Jackie thing. Before I knew it Janel starts to let out a few moans, and as I'm listening I hear some vibrating. Now I am not the

brightest candle on the cake, but it sounds to me like she's playing with herself...I hung up. Why? I really don't know why, all I know is the longer I would have stayed on that phone the harder it would have been to control myself. About twenty minutes later she texted me a smiley face emoji that reads..."I see you like to play hardball. I'll brake you." she wrote. Moments later a picture came through, a picture of the "finished product", and I'm just thinking to myself like "nah, ain't no any she just bust that phat of a but by herself. I just had to go to sleep off of that one...

K.I.M.

(Keep In Mind)

In your life understand that you will come across individuals that are placed in your life to hurt you, and individuals that are also placed in your life to help you. Each person has a purpose in your life whether it be good or bad, but trying to determine what purpose an individual serves in your life is the hard part. The closer you allow an individual get to you, its only natural that you begin to developed emotions and feelings for that person. But, the problem with that is, for one, you lack complete honesty, and with lack of honesty lies deceit, then from there temptation rises. Choosing the wrong person to invest your time and love into can be fatal to how you react to the next person that wants to get close to you and truly love you. Understandable the search for love is that of a dangerous path to follow, but know that the reward at the end of the right path will be tremendous. True, no one is perfect...but there is someone out there that is just perfect for you.

Hot Line....

After that day over the past few weeks Janel would call me on my cellphone and we would go out on a few dates, dinner, bowling, and sometimes we would even catch a movie. I felt bad going behind Bossmans back and seeing his woman even though Janel and I never had sex, it was still weird hiding a secret from a man I considered to be my best friend...

"So, are you just going to stand there, or do I have to get you undressed myself?" Janel said as she slowly made her way over to me, placing her hand on my chest working her way down and untying the string on my jogging pants. My pants fell to the floor as she slowly made her way down to her knees..."Mmmm, bigger than I remember." she said with a smile as she held my dick in her hands. She slowly wrapped her lips around the tip of as she watched me watch her. I was still shocked at the fact that she knew where I laid my head. I had never met her here nor have I ever told her. it was simply amazing watching her make my dick disappear, and even though I knew it was totally not an appropriate time to ask a question....but I had to...

"How did you know where I stay?" I asked a little strained. I watched as she slowly eased her warm juicy lips from around my dick leaving the tip of my dick on her bottom lip as she spoke...

"Well I called Jackie and asked her where you stay making it seem as if I was looking for Bossman—" she phased to kiss the tip of my dick before continuing..."I just wanted to surprise you. I hope your not mad at me." she said as she wrapped her warm lips around me again causing my thought process to crumble. She placed her hand in the center of my best pushing

my back flush against the wall. Next thing I know she starts going crazy, deepthroating me and slobbing all over my dick. I mean cleaning me up better than a vacuum cleaning up a mess with extra suction power, and it felt just as amazing as it looked...

"Janel...stop." I said. I couldn't help think about Monique, and what with us running into each other earlier today could have meant. I mean, had this been any other day before this morning and me running into Monique then Janel would have been getting nailed to a cross right now, but I couldn't do it. Every time I closed my eyes old memories of Monique would pop into my head, and those memories gave me inspiration for a hopeful future between the two of us...

"What...What's wrong L.A., did I do something wrong?" she asked as she made her way back to her feet...

"Nah...baby girl it ain't got nothing to do with you, its me. I just can't do this." I said seriously. She turned to pick up her coat before offering a response...

"There's someone else isn't there? she asked holding her coat across her forearms looking so disappointed...

"Yes and no...I'm not really certain what we are, but what I do know is she's a woman I don't want to mess things up with." I said. I grabbed her coat and helped her put it on as we walked to

the door... "She must be something special." she said. I could sense the embarrassment in her voice as she spoke and covered herself up...

"Yeah, she's really something special." I said. She leaned in and gave me a hug and followed up with a soft passionate kiss like Romeo and Juliet in their last moments together...

"She a very lucky woman to have a man like you willing to love her." she said softly. I nodded my head as I opened up the front door...

"No, actually if she chooses to be with me in would be the lucky one. But I don't know what the future holds." I said. She turned to give me another kiss, this time on the cheek...

"Well, if things for whatever reason don't work out...give me a call." she said. She walked on the porch as I replied...

"I'll be sure to take you up on that offer." I said to her. She walked to her car and before getting in she called out...

"Oh, and L.A..."

"What's up?" I asked...

"Keep this—" she was quickly interrupted as I finished what I knew would be the end of her sentence...

"Between me and you. Yeah baby girl I got you." I finished. She winked are me and a smile fell upon her face as she got into her car and drove off. As soon as I close the door my phone rings..."Hey Monique, what's up?" I answered. I could tell she had a smile on her face when she responded...

"Oh wow, I'm impressed. I see you learned how to save numbers." Monique said sarcastically. We both shared a chuckle before I responded...

"Nah, a lot of people are not that special or significant." I said. A Burt of silence filled the phone for a moment before she responded...

"I see, so Frank—" she started. She was quickly interrupted by my response...

"Damn we using government names now, MoeMoe?" I asked. she hated being called MoeMoe just as much as I hated being called Frank...

"Ugh, you know I hate that name. You play too much, L.A." she said annoyed. I laughed a little before responding with,

"Well, don't call me that name, not over these phones anyway...but what's up bighead?" I asked her.

"I'm not the one with a big head, you are!" She said in a matter of fact tone,

"Yeah, I know, I have been told that a few times." I said. She knew what I was talking about but she ignored the arrogant response.

"Anyways, I was actually calling to see if you were busy tonight. I was thinking maybe we could go on a 'pre-date' if that makes any sense." she asked. Damn, I'm supposed to be going out with Bossman, and then we gotta see Duce.

"Yeah, beautiful, unfortunately I am. Your brother called me when I made it home and asked me to go to this party with him tonight and then after that we have to go take care of some business." I said.

"Some business, huh?...Well I just was asking; I didn't really want anything. I'll just see you this weekend...or does my brother have you as well that day?" she asked. I could sense all the sarcasm in her voice, yet she was so calm...

"Nah, baby girl. I'm free that day and nothing's going to change that." I said. Even though, you never know what tomorrow will bring or if it's even promised to you; I was determined not to allow anything to get in the way of our weekend.

"Mmmhmm, yeah okay, L.A. We shall see. I'll talk to you later." she said.

"Okay beautiful." I replied. After we hung up I went to lay my clothes out for tonight, I hit the shower, and then I took a nap because clearly I have a long night ahead of me...

K.I.M.

You Can Not Force It

Love that is forced is not love at all, it is merely pain. Some say 50/50, when really, you both should give 100%, but loving someone with all of your heart is a very hard task, especially when you are not sure they will do the same. If you have to second guess whether the individual you are in a relationship with will love you back with his or her all, then it seems that you have what some would call "Poor Judgement Skills". This is when you constantly choose to be in a relationship with a person that is not really worth your time or effort to love. It's understandable that some individuals portray themselves to be something that they are not, so they trick you into loving them. Once you have been tricked into loving someone you become blinded to the "Red Flags" in the relationship, and then you fall victim to being TRAPPED. You have to realize that before that door locks and the key becomes forever lost, you must remove the blindfold and learn to pay attention to the "Tell Tale" signs that this is not the type of love you want to be subjected to. Understand that the most dreadful feeling is forcing yourself to love someone that has no intention on loving you back. True love oftentimes allow intimacy to become multiplied more effectively over time.

Money To Blow

My alarm that I set to 7:00pm had just went off. So I get up and went to go brush my teeth and wash my face before getting dressed. I got up a little early because I knew I had to iron out my new fit. While I was out at the mall today, I picked up a pair of Balmain jeans with the black and gray stitching to match my watch. I also grabbed a jet black Michael Kore's V-neck shirt with a new pair of gray Air Force Ones to top it off. I took my time and got myself ready. Before I

knew it, it was time for me to go and scoop Bossman up. I grab my keys, wallet, and jacket out of the kitchen and head toward the front door. I stop at the front closet and grab my 9mm handgun and head out of the door. Bossman and I have a meeting with Duce tonight. I can never be too careful, not after what happened the last time. I get in the car and toss my jacket on the backseat, place my gun in the center armrest console, then I pull off. I pulled up to Bossman's house and I see him standing on his porch with the biggest grin on his face, finishing up his cigarette. He turns to lock the door and then makes his way over to the passenger side door.

"L.A. baby, what's good?" he asked. He seemed to be in a good mood, better than usual.

"I'm good, fool. What you so damn happy about?" I asked. He slouched down in the seat and took a deep breath before responding...

"Maaann, you pulled up right in time. Janel had just left to go back to work. Her boss had let her get a two hour lunch break because she had to work a double. So she came home and fucked the shit out of me. I'm not sure what had gotten into her but she was sucking and ridding me like I was a random nigga in the streets. It was crazy man. I guess she got tired of holding out from me for like the past few weeks. As a matter of fact, I think the last time we had sex was like a few days after that little get together Jackie and Cell threw." he said. Could it have been the fact that I turned Janel down that had her all juiced up and wanting to fuck?...Its possible.

"Uh, Bossman, so whose party is this?" I asked. His physical excitement evenly matched his eager response.

"Aw man, its this little cold chicks party I meet on Facebook. She had tagged me in her post about a tattoo party. After that, we started talking and she asked me to swing through." he said. Now any other time, I would have been eager to get to a party full of females shaking their ass or getting tattoos, but the only thing that's on my mind is his sister, Monique, and how I would have better enjoyed myself if I was with her. When we pulled up to the house, I got this cold chill that ran down my back. The block was a dead end. It was dark by this time and the block was poorly lit, even though there were other cars parked on the street and the house was lit up, full of people, and the music was rocking, I still had a feeling something wasn't right. So as Bossman got out of the car I grabbed my gun out o the armrest console and glued it to my hip...

"Hey Bossman...I'm glad you could make it." a voice called out from the doorway of the house. As we approached the house there stood a beautiful five foot three, caramel toned young lady who seemed to *have some Italian in her. She had long hair, apple green eyes, a nice body, and a gorgeous smile...*

"Hey beautiful." Bossman said as he leaned in for a hug and a kiss. She then turned her attention to me...

"And who is this handsome devil you got with you?" she asked. Bossman then turned his attention to me as he wrapped his arms around her waist...

"Kayla this is my boy L.A.. L.A. this is Kayla." Bossman said. I reached my hand out only to embrace hers...

"Pleasure to meet you Kayla." I said...

"Nice to meet you as well. Well y'all don't just stand there come on in." Kayla said. Now despite the rough looking neighborhood the inside of the house was nice..."You want anything to drink honey?" Kayla asked Bossman as she firmly leaned against his chest...

"Yeah baby, just bring me a Budlite, I can't be drinking too heavy tonight. I got some business to take care of later." Bossman said. She nodded her head and then turned her attention to me...

"And L.A., what about you?" she asked. I was already not feeling to comfortable about being here so I'm just really trying to be aware of my surroundings. On top of that Bossman and I have a meeting with Duce, and I have no idea what it is about...

"I'll just take a pop or a bottle of water." I said. Her reaction to my response seemed a little hesitant as she walked away...

"L.A. man what's up? Why you seem so tense?" Bossman asked. I stepped over to Bossmans side and leaned in...

"Man I'm just not getting a good vibe about being here." I said in a low voice. For whatever reason Bossman took my seriousness as a joke...

"L.A., man relax...I don't see his you not getting a good vibe, look over there—" his hand pointed over to the living room as he continued "Do you not see all that ass shaking, women dancing and getting drunk...or look at her—" he then turned my attention to a gorgeous

young lady sitting in the tattoo chair getting a butterfly tattoo done right below her panty line as he went on..."See, and she's just asking to show off her goodies. Ima need you to tighten up and get with

the program. Have a few drinks, loosen up a little." he said. Even though Bossman had a point, I should be having fun and enjoying myself, I just couldn't bring myself to do so. Tonight was just one of those nights. Kayla returned with the drinks and when she returned she had a young lady with her...

"L.A. this is my friend Erica. Erica this is L.A." Kayla said. We reached out for each others hand and simultaneously spoke...

"Its nice to meet you—.." The room seemed to have fell silent for a moment. Erica was every bit of five foot five and about 160 lbs, dark skinned with braces. She had short hair with a skin tight dress on that created the illusion o being naked, helped by the lighting in the room we were in. She wasn't my type at all, but was anybody my type in comparison to Monique...

"Well, we will just leave you two to get better acquainted." Kayla said. Bossman protested as be

and Kayla walked away. I watched as Kayla took Bossman by his hand and led him up the stair case and into a room. My attention was quickly placed on Erica as I heard her speak...

"So...I don't see a girl on your side , nor do I see a ring on your finger. So I'm assuming you came alone.?" Erica asked. Uninterested in her flirtatious manner my response was dry...

"Yeah, my boy drug me along." I answered. She took a sip from her plastic red cup and muttered...

"Hey, follow me." she said softly. She took my hand and guided me to the back indoor patio..."Sit...sit..." she insisted as she patted the padded cushion on the futon. I took a seat a nice distance away from her, but she didn't hesitate to fill that gap. She placed her hand on my knee and even though she thought I didn't notice her easing her way

up my leg, I did. I removed her hand and placed it in her lap and replaced that awkward moment of silence with a question...

"So where is your man?" I asked her. The question lingered in the air for a moment as she took another sip from her cup...

"I'd rather not waste time talking about that situation." she said as she crossed her legs leaning in a little closer. I gently placed my hand on her shoulder...

"Erica...do you love him?" I asked. She was very hesitant to answer the question rudely laughing it off until she saw my face and sensed that my question had sincerity behind it. Shethe straightened up her posture and offered an answer to the question...

"Yeah...yeah I do." she said. I placed my hand ontop of hers as I spoke...

"So if you love him why are you throwing yourself at a man that you don't even know? I don't understand..." I said confused. The question seemed to make her a little emotional. I could feel her pain as she spoke...

" Yeah I love him but I'm not sure I want to be with him after he cheated on me with this bitch Sabrina.—" She wiped what surely was a tear from the corner of her eye as she continued. "I gave this man the best two years of my life only to be stepped on, and honestly I want him to feel what I feel." she said as she leaned in to type and kiss me but was quickly stopped...

"Erica, stop...this isn't what you truly want to do, nod can I allow you to." I said. As tears ran from her eyes down to her chin I gently wiped them away with the tips of my thumbs. Cupping her chin as I continued..."Listen sweetheart, I know your hurting, your angry, and you just want to replace that hurt and anger with revenge...Its not worth it. You seem like a good person, therefore he is the one losing out, not you. Getting even or trying to get even only makes you just as bad of a person as he is and as a woman your devaluing yourself. And if you devalue

yourself how can you expect a man to value you?" I questioned. She looked a me with sad puppy dog like eyes and said...

"So what should I do?" she asked.

"I'm not going to tell you what to do, but what I will say is if you stay your only showing him that what he did was acceptable. You deserve a man that will love and cherish you like the Queen that you are." I said. A slight smile fell upon her face...

"And why hasn't some one snatched you up yet?" she asked in a joking manner as she continued "Can I call you sometime?" she asked...

"Well to answer your question, I haven't come across anyone worth giving the world to. And to your second question, sure, but I'm telling you now I'm just looking for a friendship." I said. She pulled out her phone and shrugged her shoulders...

"That's fine, what's your number?" Erica asked. Now as I'm giving Erica my number I hear the music stop and a lot of commotion coming from up stairs, so I go to check it out...

"I'll be right back." I told Erica. As I make my way through the herd of people cluttering the staircase I see Bossman standing other with his shirt and shoes off and his pants half fastened exchanging a few heated words with another guy. So I intervene..."Wow, wow, wow, hey broth a what's going on. What seems to be the problem? I asked hurriedly. The guy pushed me to the side and said...

"This ain't got shit to do with you." the guy said. I catch my balance and I step back in front of Bossman. From my periphery I could clearly see Kayla peaking into the hallway from behind the bathroom door. Instantly I knew it had something to do with her...

"Listen, whatever beef you got with him I'm sure is not worth fighting over." I said trying to calmly defuse the situation...

"This piece of shit was fucking my girl—" he was saying. I glanced over at Bossman who had a grin on his face, then turned back to this angry man as he continued..."And yo bitch ass has the nerve to try and defend him." he said angrily. He turned to a group of four guys that

had just made their way up the steps asking what happened..."Man this punk bitch right here slept with Kayla and this douche bag next to him decides to step in like captain save a hoe." Before he could continue I had interrupted...

"Hey, for one my guy, that "Punk Bitch" you referring to is my boy, and if he fucked yo girl oh well take a number, you should be dealing with her and not him. And second, I have not once disrespected you in any way and I would be damned if I stand here and continue to allow you to disrespect me and my boy." I said seriously. His tone was very aggressive as he spoke... "You and yo boy can get y'all ass beat." he said. Right at that moment I knew two things. One, shit was about to get ugly, and two, this is what that bad vibe I have been feeling all night must have been. As the guy and his gang start to approach I clearly see that we are outnumbered. So I pulled out my gun and took aim at the head of the alpha male leading the pack of blood thirsty wolves. A collective "Whohhh!" came out of the mouths of the attackers as well as the crowd of people gathered on the staircase. Before my father was murdered hob would always tell me never to use a gun, but if I had to, don't ever up the mag and not pull the trigger. But I had no choice...

"Listen brother, we not looking for any trouble—" I was saying, but I was interrupted by the sound of Kayla's voice rushing over between us as she turned and looked the man in his eyes...

"T-Mac please...please just go." she said. T-Mac kept his eyes on me and my pistol as he took a few steps back...

"Its all good...I'll catch you on the rebound." he said to me. They turned and walked away down the steps in the distance. I could here T-Mac yell out "You better watch yo back boy.". I felt a gentle touch graze across my cheek...It was Erica, and in a soft tone...

"L.A....can you put that away please.." she said. I put the gun away and quickly turned my attention to Bossman...

"Man get yo shit on now, we up." I said seriously. He hurried to the restroom and grabbed the rest of his clothing, then we both made our way downstairs...

"I am so sorry you guys, I didn't think he would have came." Kayla said as she walked us to the door. in the background I hear Erica...

"Bye L.A., I'll shoot you a text when I make it home. Thank you!" she said. She might have thought I was rude for not responding back to her but I was just focused on my surroundings and getting the hell out of the area. As I make it to my car door I turn to see Bossman and Kayla standing near the porch kissing...

"Man get the fuck in the car!" I said more than irritated. They shared one quick peck and then he jogged over to the car and got in. We pulled off and the only thing that's going through my mind is what would have happened if I let Bossman come by himself to that party."...

"Yo, L.A. man that shit was crazy!" he said joking. It angered me a little to see him taking what just happened as a joke...

"You knew she had a boyfriend didn't you?" I asked. He nodded his head in conformation as I continued..."Have you lost yo damn mind?" I asked seriously. He responded quickly with a witty remark...

"Clearly my mind is in place, your the one that upped the mag on him and his whole crew. Why would you bring that out with you anyway knowing we gotta see Duce? he asked. He was right, there was no way in hell I was going to get past Duce's guards with a pistol...

"For one, I already had a bad vibe about tonight, and clearly sticking with my first mind was right. And second you can't be too safe with Duce, especially not after what happened last time." I said. The last time Duce requested to see Bossman and I it was a few years ago and that didn't go well. Bossman ended up shorting Duce's cut thinking that he wouldn't notice. Well, he

did. When he found out he called me and Bossman and told us to meet him at Casper's place which was nothing more than a cemetery *that Duce owned. To make a long story short, Bossman ended up coming clean about what he had done and after Duce had broken three fingers on Bossmans right hand and burned the back of my neck with a cigar. He made us both get down on our knees as he pointed his gun at us and said..."I will kill you both, and not lose an*

hour of sleep." Just like I didn't know back then Bossman was skimming off the top, I have no idea now why he wants to see us after all this time...

"Yeah, you right." Bossman said as he rubbed his left hand across his right hand as if remembering the pain of the broken bones. He continued..."But I know for a fact his money has been on point since then, if not always extra." he said. We were both clueless about a meeting with the devil that was scheduled at 11:15pm which was about ten minutes away...

K.I.M.

Sex

Have you really ever noticed something about sex? I mean other than the fact that it is an amazing feeling, it goes a little deeper then that...ha, no pun intended. Sex is considered a sin that we all partake in at some point in our lives, some earlier than others. Once those doors are penetrated there is an inner beast that is let loose, and truthfully, the hunger of that beast must be fed. The crazy part is, you never really know at first how far you are willing to go to reach that maximum peak to climax. You are open to new ideas and desires, from handcuffs and whips, to sex games in trips (3's). I am not one to judge because we have all had our wild times just

"Living in the moment", but once you elevate your state of mind you come to a realization that sex is nothing more than an addiction. Like any other addiction, its only good for the moment. Realize this before its too late (for ladies that means before your walls come crumbling down beyond repair, and for the fellas that means before even the strongest pill won't help get you up). Making love is a passion that is so much more fulfilling than anything you have ever imagined, and can last a lifetime. Your body is a temple. After so many "backstage passes" your value becomes tarnished. Remember everything that looks good is not good for you, and just because there is candy displayed in front of you, don't mean you have to take it...

Deal or No Deal

When we pulled up to Casper's place, something told me that this was not an ordinary meeting. The last time we met Duce here it was three SUVs surrounding his limo. This time there was not limo and only one black SUV. My phone rings..."Hello?" I answered. A deep voice replied...

"The boss wants you to follow us." The lights of the SUV flicked on and the engine revved up...

"Follow you where exactly?" I asked. The phone hung up without an answer to my question. Bossman turned his attention to me as the SUV passed by the car and I started after it...

"Who, where are we going? In thought we were meeting Duce here?" Bossman asked. It seemed that my pulse started to grow faint just thinking about what would happen tonight. Every thought ended badly...

"I'm not sure where we are going, all I know is Duce wants to meet with us and clearly he don't want us to know where or why." I answered. I could see all of the worry that started to haunt Bossman as he slumped down in his seat. I wasn't sure if it was just me, but this ride was one of the longest rides of my life. The whole ride I'm just thinking to myself about Monique and giving up this lifestyle and do

something more productive with my life...but what? We finally make it to

our destination. We were definitely not in the city anymore. We pulled into this U-shaped driveway right in front of a beautiful pearl walkway that led to the front door of Duce's mansion. My heart skipped a beat as I watched the goons we were following hop out of the SUV with automatic assault rifles that looked like AKs and SKs and head in our direction. I heard Bossman swallow hard as he opened up the passenger side door...

"Follow me." the goon that was driving demanded. Now I really knew something was off. No pat down, no car search, no scanner for any wires...why were we here? I asked myself. As we approached the house the front door swings open, and Duce is standing in the doorway arms open with the biggest smile on his face...

"Bossman, L.A... I'm glad to see you made it!" he proclaimed. Bossman and I looked at each other confused as Duce gave us both a warm greeting into his home..."Come, come make yourselves at home." Duce said. We followed Duce into his home where he led us to the kitchen. From the little of the house that I saw as we made our way to the kitchen was absolutely eloquent; marble floors, diamond shaped chandeliers, and lots of fine China..."Would you boys like something to drink?" Duce asked as he made his way around the bar table...

"No, no thank you." me and Bossman said simultaneously. He wasn't taking no for an answer...

"Come on now boys have a drink with me, this is a night for celebration!" he said as he poured out three glasses of whiskey...

"With all due respect Duce, the last time we saw you it wasn't a good thing, so excuse me for not being in a celebratory mood...Why exactly are we here?" I asked seriously. Duce didn't seem to be appalled by my rudeness at all...

"Yeah L.A., your right, the last time we saw each other ya boy Bossman here was stealing from me,...but that was then and this is now. Despite that ancient mistake that was made you two have helped skyrocket my success and wealth. I'm not sure how you did it but you two have singlehandedly, over the past three years, brought in well over 13.8 million dollars." Duce said. As he took a sip from his glass it gave me that opportunity to ask...

"So, what exactly does that have to do with us? That sounds like good news for you and all, but I'm still trying to figure out what that has to do with why we are here." I said. He sampled his fingers pointing them in my direction as he spoke...

"See I knew there was something I liked about you. You remind me so much of myself, all about business and straight to the point. Well, I have brought you two here tonight to make you an offer—" Duce said. He was quickly interrupted by Bossmans timely outburst...

"What kind of offer?" he asked. Duce smiled as he poured himself another glass of whiskey...

"Well boys I am looking to expand to another country, but I need someone to take over my empire here. Which is where you two come in at. You both are young, smart, and got that hustler mentality. Most importantly I see the potential in you both to be great leaders." he said...

"So basically you want us to continue rolling for you." I said in a matter of fact tone. His response though was quick...

"No, not at all. If that was the case that could have been a conversation we would have had over the phone. I brought you both here tonight, into my home to give you the opportunity of a lifetime. I want y'all to take over here as my partners." Duce said seriously. Bossmans eyes widened as Duce continued to speak..."My offer, if you choose to tame it comes with four out of the eleven mansions I have, two for both of you, all access to my clientele and workers." he said. The deal sounded good but it had to have a catch...

"Yeah, so what's in it for you? I asked, doubting that there were any good intentions behind this offer.

"Well L.A., other than twelve percent each month being deposited into my bank account there's really not much I looking to gain. I'm just at a point in my life where I just want to sit back and watch my money do backflips." he said. Duce clapped his hands together as if he knew he had us in the bag..."So what do you say fellas...do we have a deal?" Dave asked. Bossman looked over at me soulless as if he wanted to scream out "NO!", but he remained quiet...

"I'm not really sure Duce. I mean it sounds like a great opportunity but—" I was saying as Dave cut in...

"Listen L.A., you and Bossman don't have to answers right this minute. I have set up my last deal three weeks from today, so I will give you a week and a half to get back at me with an answer. That should give you enough time to think my offer over, but in the meantime—" Duce said as he walked over to one of the table drawers and tossed Bossman and I both a set of keys as he walked us back to the front door and outside..." You two enjoy your new little toys." He said. He then turned our attention toward two full loaded twin Ferraris. Both were triple black with limo tinted windows sitting on some black on black four Giotto's. Before I knew it Bossman was already inside his checking out everything...

"This is nice and all Duce, but I can't take this." I said. He laid his hand on my shoulder as he began to speak...

"Nonsense L.A., if anything you earned that. Just think of it as a bonus, and trust me, if you choose to take on this partnership there's a lot more where that came from. Besides, how do you plan on getting home?" he asked. I quickly took a look around and my car was nowhere to in sight...

"Duce where is my car?!" I cried out. He could sense the discomfort in my voice...

"Take it easy cowboy, its actually on its way to your house as we speak" he said. A cold chill ran down my back at the thought of him knowing where I stay...

"How do you know where I live?!" I asked. A grin fell upon his face as he spoke...

"I know more about you than you think I do Frank. When your a man in my position you make it your business to know everything there is to know about a person before you just hand over everything you have worked so hard for." he said. In my mind I wasn't sure I Duce had just become a friend or a dangerous for. As he walked back into his humble home I swiftly made my way over to Bossman...

"Get in the car and go straight to my house now." I said seriously. Bossman nodded his head as he revved up the engine and pulled off. I get inside my Ferrari and I instantly notice all the leather interior with the initials L.A. detailed into it. This was more than just a bonus, this car was a contract. I pull up to my house and my jeep was sitting in front of the house and Bossman is just now pulling into my driveway behind me. Bossman hops out the car smoking a blunt...

"L.A. baby what's up man, why you look so tense?" he said as he tried passing me the blunt...

"Well let's see, for one I once again put myself in the middle of some shit to help you because you want to be careless and reckless. We just gat a target painted on our head all because you want to be careless and selfish and mess with a chick you already knew was taken." I said with irritation...

"Aww man L.A., you talking about them niggas from the part? Bro they ain't gone do shit man, them niggas was just playing man." Bossman joked. I smacked the blunt from his hands and grabbed him by his collar as I rammed his back into the side of the house...

"Name one mutherfucka in the city that gets a gun shoved in their face and say they gonna get you and don't...name one nigga in the streets that play like that!" I said angrily. With Bossmans high now blown

I could clearly see the reality of the chaos he caused start to settle in on him. As I released the tight grip from around the collar of his shirt Bossman stood puzzled, motionless, and damn near speechless. The only words he was able to muster up was...

"You right L.A., man you right." he said somewhat ashamed. I could tell his nerves were getting him. He pulled out a cigarette. His hands were shaking tying to light it. He gave a sigh of relief once he finally got it lit. He continued while blowing smoke off into the air...changing the subject..."So what are we going to do about this offer of Duces?" he asked . The piercing look I gave him could have torn straight through him as I spoke..

"The better question is how in the hell does Duce know where I stay?" I asked seriously. I saw his Addams Apple jolt as he struggled to swallow before speaking...

"Well, he...he said he wanted to keep tabs on you and make sure you didn't go anywhere, you know after what happened the last time we met with Duce, he thought you might try to retaliate. But I told him you wasn't like that man...but he insisted for "Just in Case" reasons. Bossman admitted. I stood there with this look of utter disgrace and I was honestly debating on whether I would slap the dog shit out of him or just let it go...I threw my hands up in the air as I reluctantly posed a rhetorical question...

"So I guess that's how he knows my real damn name as well huh?" I asked. All Bossman did was nod his head in conformation to the question. I turned my back to him to unlock my side screen door..."Leave...Just go man." I said tiredly. I could hear the sourness in the tone of his voice as he spoke...

"L.A. man come on you—" he began saying as his plea was stopped short by the sound of my side door shutting in his face as I stepped inside. I didn't see him but I heard Bossman peel off after he pulled out of my driveway. It wasn't the first time we got into it and it

probably wouldn't be the last, but he was wrong, and he had no right to be mad.

K.I.M.

You Can't Change A Person
There is a huge difference between molding an individual and trying to change an individual. In life you have gone through trials and tribulations that has ultimately made you into the man or woman that you are today. True, most of those hurdles you have had to overcome, in the moment may have seemed impossible to get over, but you made it. You can always mold a person, your lover, or spouse, but you can never change them. True indeed your words and actions may have an impact on their life in the most positive way, but without the desire for themselves to change, they won't change. In order for your quest for love to be successful you must be able to accept a person for who they are and help guide and mold them to the reality of themselves. They may have their flaws but remember you have some as well, and with every flaw lies potential. You will not see the same potential in every person that you choose to be with, nor will they see the same in you. See this nine letter word is so powerful because it unlocks doors that give you that opportunity for growth and development, eventually molding those flaws into works of art. POTENTIAL is defined as the capability of coming into being or action, which basically means with flaws comes potential, and its only through potential, that success can be at its highest.

Saturday

"If your ready sweetheart I can be on my way." I said to Monique...

"Yeah, I'm ready." Monique responded. It was a little early and our reservation for dinner wasn't scheduled until 9 o'clock, so Monique and I had about an hour and a half to burn, which was fine with me. That extra hour or so will only allow us to opportunity to spend more time together...

"Okay cool, I'll be there in about thirty minute." I said...

"Okay see you then." she replied. Even though I was already in her area because I had to go and pick up my suit for our date tonight. I had to buy myself a little more time so that I can go and buy Monique some fresh picked roses from Bob florist...

"L.A baby, what's going on!" the florist said. When I walked into the flower shop Hus voice was the only one I heard...

"Bobby, my main man, what's going on? How's business?" I asked. He came from behind the counter and greeted me with open arms, literally. See Bobby is Italian, so he's all off into that whole "touchy greeting" that's a part of his culture. He's well into his mid fifties and he's only about five foot five, short but the heart of a tiger...

"L.A. my man, business is just fine.—" he was saying as he leaned in a little closer in a joking manner..."How is that beautiful mother of yours?" he asked...

"Watch ya self Bobby." I said. We laughed as I placed my hand on his shoulder walking him back over to the counter as I continued..."But all jokes aside, she's doing fine, thanks for asking." I said...

"No problem at all," he said as he made his way around the counter, then continuing..."So...its not Valentine's day, nor is it your mothers birthday, and I know you didn't just drop by to see me looking that

t sharp. So who's the special lady?" he said. I'm quite sure Bobby noticed the slight grin that had fallen upon my face...

"Damn Bobby am I really that predictable?" I asked. We both laughed as Bobby offered a response to my question...

"Not predictable yeah, more so concrete in your ways...So...Who is the lucky lady?" Bobby asked. After Bobby grabbed the two dozen roses from the glass showcase a moment of silence filled the air as he looked at me waiting for a response to his question...

"Monique." I said. A bewildering look captured capture his face. He stopped wrapping the flowers and the words started to fumble out of his mouth...

"Monique?...Lil Monique?... MoeMoe?" he asked surprised. I nodded my head in confirmation as he continued..."But...but that's Bossmans sister." he stuttered out. I placed my index finger to my lips as I spoke...

"Yes it is...Which is why this conversation between us never happened." I said seriously. I pulled out three hundred dollars and slid it across the counter as I continued..."I'm sure has a reasonable secret we can keep between us." I said to him. Bobby smiled as he grabbed the

money and continued wrapping the flowers up...

"What secret you talking about L.A.?" he said airily. He winked his left eye at me as he handed

me the flowers...

"See Bobby, that's why your my man." I said. He stepped from behind the counter to walk me to the door...

"You kids enjoy yourselves tonight." Bobby said patting me on my shoulder as walked out the door. A few moments later I pulled up to Monique's place. I hop out and walk up to the door and ring the doorbell. I his the flowers behind my back before she opened the door. An Angel is what she reminded me of the way the light hit her glowing body in the doorway. She had on this dark red dress that fit her to the T. The dress was long but had a slit going up from the bottom up to

her mid thigh and her back was out. What really topped it off was the fact that she had a natural glow, no makeup but red eyeliner. I was lost for words as I admired her beauty...

"I still have to put on my heels. Your welcome to come in you know." Monique said. I finally snapped back into reality...

"Yeah, that's fine....here, these are for you." I said as I pulled the flowers from behind my back and handed them to her. Her smile started to light up the dim sky...

"Aww L.A., thank you." she said sweetly. She pulled me in and gave me a warm hug..."I have to put these in some water." she said. She swiftly made her way to the kitchen. I followed and watched as she separated the flowers by the bottles and placed them I. to vases accordingly...

"Monique...you look absolutely beautiful." I said seriously. Filling up the last vase she paused and turned her attention toward me and spoke...

"Thank you L.A., you look damn good yourself...You know you didn't have to get me those flowers." she said as she placed the last vase on the counter and made her way to the living room...

"Nonsense, you are a queen, and you deserve to be treated as such." I said. I saw a slight grin touch her cheeks as she was putting on her heels...

"Oooo...okay, so Mr. L.A. when did you become the Romeo type?" she asked. I helped Monique to her feet and pulled her close to me as I spoke in a soft, baritone voice...

"I've always had it in me, I was just missing my Juliet." I said. The room seemed to have gotten hotter. We stood face to face, chest to chest. Each time she inhaled I could feel her heartbeat grow stronger each second. She took a step back and cleared her throat...

"So where are we going to eat?" she asked...

"El Ralston. Its a Greek restaurant...Greek still is your favorite isn't it?" I asked as I helped Monique onto her trench coat...

"Yeah, actually it is...How did you know that?" she asked curiously...

"I remember your brother always complaining about you always cooking Greek foods." I said as we made it to and out of the front door...

"I see you have a good memory...that's good." she said. We both walked over to the passenger side and I opened up her door and helped her in. As soon as I got in she said...

"So I see you not riding around in ya flashy new Ferrari like my brother. What is this a 2012 Magnum?...Nice, real low key." she said. I started up the car and a seeded her multiple questions...

"Yeah its a Magnum, and the difference between your brother and I is that he feels as though he needs to flashy to impress people. Me on the other don't give a damn what the next person thinks, nor do I care to try and impress a person." I said confidently. She smiled and pulled down the sun blocker and opened the mirror compartment to apply a dark red lipstick...

"Well I'm impressed...but you don't care right." she asked. Before I was given the opportunity to reply to her statement my phone rings...

"Wow, we speaking of the devil, its your brother. My Bluetooth in the car is hooked up, so try and be quiet." I said. I hit the button on my steering wheel to answer the phone...

"Sup." Bossman said...

"What's up Bossman?" I asked...

"L.A. man what's going on?" he countered...

"Nothing much just doing me." I replied...

"Hey listen man I know we ain't been on good term these past couple of days but I found a way to make it up. Man come to this party over here on Abington St." he said. The music in the background started to die down...

"Nah, man I'm good. I'm actually on my way to dinner with a beautiful young lady." I said. I could hear him smacking his lips...

"Come on man really, you gonna pick some bitch over ya bro?" he said. I turned my attention toward Monique. I saw her trying not to laugh listening to her brother talk...

"Hey man, watch ya mouth, shes not just bitch. She's something way more meaningful." I said seriously. My eyes once again bared witness to her beauty while we were at a light...

"So you just gone ditch me for some chick you probably barely know?" he said sounding hurt. Trying my hardest to not just blurt out the truth that I'm out with his sister I settle for a different response...

"You don't know what I know." I said. With a sarcastic chuckle he swiftly responded...

"Oh yeah...so what do you know?" He asked sarcastically. As soon as those words finished traveling through my speakers I could feel Monique's beautiful eyes on me eager to hear what I had to say...

"Well, if you must know...I know that she's absolutely beautiful, smart and Loving. I know that her favorite color is purple, her favorite food style is Greek. I know that as a child she didn't have a father, someone in her life she could feel protected by. And I know that I care about her." I said. Out of the corner of my eye I can see a smile fall upon Monique's face and her cheeks began to redden...

"Yeah, yeah, yeah captain save a how. I don't hear anything different that separates that one from..." he was saying as he was quickly cut short by the sound o the dial tone, when I hung up...

"I'm...I'm sorry I—" I started to say. Cut off by her angel like voice...

"L.A. there's no need to apologize, he's my brother. If anything I should be apologizing to you." she said. We both let out a laugh as she continued..."He is and always will be a dog. He treats women like they're just disposable creatures. I'm just glad his ignorant ways didn't latch on to you." he said. Little did she know watching how Bossman performed in his relationships helped me to see how NOT to treat a woman...

"Well don't give me to much credit. I'm not an Angel. I've had my wild days in the past...But it was because of those wild days that I was able to truly appreciate and value a woman's worth. I wasn't always the man you see today." I said. As those words left the tip of my tongue and escaped passed my lips, I had pulled into the valet section of the street in front of the building. One valet worker came to my door as the other attended to Monique...

"Good evening sir, welcome to the El Ralston." the young valet worker announced as he climbed in to my car and pulled off. Monique takes me by the arm as I lead her into the building...

"Wow...this place is so beautiful." she said in wonder. She wasn't lying, the place had glass chandeliers, red velvet carpet, and a beautiful waterfall in the middle of the room. To top it off the aroma was right on point...

"Yeah it is, but compared to you I hadn't really noticed." I said. She hugged my arm a little tighter with a smile as we approached the host...

"Ah, good evening sir, madam. I assume a table for two?" he said...

"Yes actually I have reservations. "I responded...

"The name please sir." the host said...

"L.A." I said. The tall and slim man looked down at his clipboard full of names for a quick second before finding mine...

"Ah, okay here we are. Please if you would so kindly follow me I'll seat you two." he said respectfully. We had what seemed to me to be the best seat in the house, right next to the waterfall..."Your waiter will be here momentarily, in the meantime her are your menus...enjoy."

the host said. Monique and I shared a brief moment of silence as we both admired the elegant restaurant...

"Hello my name is Amanda, I am your waitress this evening." the waitress said. I could tell she took pride in her job. She continued..."If you two are all set I'll be happy to take your order." She said. The waitress pulled out her pen and pad as I spoke...

"Yes, actually we are ready. We'll have a bottle of your finest wine. I'll have a steak gyro and she will have a chicken Sw orma with a Greek salad side for both." I said. The veteran waitress repeated back the order to the T, and with a slight nod of my conformation she dashed off leaving Monique and I alone with each other. She sat there looking at me with a puzzled yet amazed look in her eyes...

"Monique, is everything alright?" I asked. She leaned forward in her seat and said...

"How did you know—" she began. I already know what her question was so I decided to finish her sentence for her...

"Chicken Sworma was your favorite?...I have my sources." I said with a smile on my face...

"You seem to be able to get a lot of information out of my brother about me without putting two and two together." she said. I let out a laugh as I noticed the waitress making her way back to the table with the wine and a bucket of ice...

"Well no offense but your brother isn't the brightest candle on the cake when he's under the influence." I said. The waitress made it to the table withe the wine, glasses, and a bucket of ice...

"Here are your drinks, your food should be ready momentarily." the waitress said. The waitress started to walk away, but then quickly made her way back over to the table..."I'm sorry for sticking my nose where it doesn't belong, but I just have to know...How long have you two been married?" the waitress asked. The question brought a giggle out of Monique and almost made me choke on the wine. Monique and I both looked at each other. I could have answered, but

really this was a good time for me to see how Monique looked at me. With my attention still on Monique I tilted my glass toward her and said...

"No, your fine Amanda. Go ahead honey, you can answer Amanda's question." Monique sat there with this shy smile as she spoke...

"Actually we are not married, just very...very good friends seeing where life takes us." Monique said. Amanda crossed her arms in disbelief...

"Wow that's too bad, you two look like you would make a good couple." she said. Monique and I shared a smile together as we watched Amanda swiftly depart from the table. I waited until Monique raised her glass to her lips to bombard her with a question we were both anticipating me to ask...

"Very good friends huh? I asked. She finished her sip of wine And then offered a response...

"Did I say something wrong? I mean, we are very good friends, and we are seeing where life takes us. And regardless to what happens with us I always want to be able to maintain a friendship." Monique said. Even though I understand exactly what she meant, I was still a little lost on how she felt about me...until she started to speak again..."Don't get me wrong L.A. I like you, am I care for you a lot. But, I'm just not sure I want a man that lives your type of lifestyle."

she said. The waitress then returned to the table with our food...

"Here's the Chicken Sworma for you—". she placed the plate in front of Monique, "and the Steak Gyro for you. Is there anything else I can do for you two?" Amanda asked. Both Monique and I shook our heads no and once again the waitress was off...

"My type of lifestyle... what exactly is my type of lifestyle?" I asked. Monique took her sheer silk napkin and placed it on her lap as she answered my question with a question...

"You still work with my brother right?" she asked...

"Yeah, why?" I asked. She shook her head.

"That's the lifestyle I don't want. I don't know about the other women you've dated, but I don't want that lifestyle where I don't know if today is the last time I will see you, or a lifestyle where we have to have visiting hours because your locked up...I worry enough about my

brother. Well I did before I found out he's working for his father." she said. I couldn't believe my ears...

"Wait, what?...You mean to tell me Duce is Bossmans father?...How do you even know that?" I thought y'all pops left y'all!" I said surprised. I could see Monique's eyes begin to glisten with tears as she spoke...

"L.A., you have to promise me you won't tell my brother." she said. I grabbed her hands and held them inside I mine...

"Monique I promise." I said...

"I found out a few years ago before I went off to college, my mother told me. It all came out because I wanted to go to college, but you know my didn't have that type of money. So when I told her that I didn't score high enough on my SATs to get a full ride we were both devastated. So a few days later I overhear her on the phone telling this man that his daughter wanted to go to college and how she didn't want me to end up like her or worst. She told him how much it would be to send me and they set up a time the next day for him to come by the house to drop off the money. That next day came and I was in my room. James was out as usual but I heard a mans voice so I knew it had to be the man my mother was on the phone with. I rushed downstairs and there he stood. My mother tried to play it off and any it was one of her old classmates just stopping by, but I knew better. So I asked him if he was my father...He and my mother looked at each other, and to make a long story short they told me the truth but made me swear to keep that secret form my brother. But it was only under two conditions. One being him putting me through college and the other being him looking after my brother...and so far he has kept his word, so I have kept mine." she said seriously. It was so much going through my head at the moment it was crazy. So this whole time the man Bossman looked at as a father figure,

was actually his father, and Duce knew that was his son. Wait..then that also means that not only am I going behind Bossmans back by taking his sister out but I'm also crossing the line with someone more dangerous. I was literally lost for words and Monique could tell, which is why I believe she excused herself from the table...

"L.A., I'm sorry, would you excuse me, I have to fix myself back up. You don g) me all teary eyed." she said. She got up and walked toward the ladies room, and as soon as she was out of sight, Amanda walks over to the table...

"How are you enjoying your meal?" Amanda asked...

"It's fine Amanda, thanks for checking." I answered. She leaned in a little closer...

"Not a problem. Would you like any desert?" she asked...

"Nah, actually I didn't see anything I was interested in, but thanks." I said. She leaned in a little closer and spoke in a more whispered tone...

"Well from what I'm told strawberries and ice cream goes great together on top of me." she said devilishly. She wrote down her number and placed the piece of paper inside my right jacket pocket as she continued..."If things don't work out give me a call." she said. I felt as if I was in the twilight zone because as soon as Amanda walked away Monique came right around the corner...

"Everything okay sweetheart?" I asked as I stood and pulled her chair out...

"Yeah I'm fine, I guess I always though it would hurt less knowing who my father was. But really it was less painful when I didn't know." she said. I took her hand in mine and kissed it. I didn't want the rest of the night to be a downer so I figured I would lighten up the mood...

"Sooo...guess what." I said. She looked at me with a tiny smile on her face...

"What?" she replied. I took out the number from my pocket and handed it to her..."What's this?" she asked...

"The waitress's number. She gave it to me when you walked away." I said. Monique started laughing...

"Awww, that's so cute. She got a little crush on you—" she said playfully. She waved the number in front of me as she continued..."So...when you gonna call her?" she asked. I snatched the paper from her, balled it up and dropped it in the ice bucket now full of water next to us...

"Why would I waste my tine when I have someone far more valuable right in front of me." I said. Monique's cheeks were cherry red and her eyes seemed to be dancing to the beat of my heart. We continued eating and chatting. It was like we were kids all over again infatuated with knowing more about each other. Then her phone rings. It was an unfamiliar number so she ignored it. Moments later it rang again...

"L.A. I'm sorry—" she said...

"No, your fine, take the call." I urged. I poured me another glass of wine as she answered the phone...

"Hello...Yes, yes this is she—" Monique said. I could tell something was wrong the way her posture straightened and her demeaned changed..."What...are you serious!...Oh my God, is he okay?!...I'm on my way." she said worriedly. She hung up the phone, struggling to put it back in her purse because she was trembling...

"Monique, what's going on... is everything okay?" I asked with concern. She shook her head no quickly bringing her hands to her eyes to wipe away the tears...

"James is in the hospital. He's been shot." she said. A flow of numbness quickly ran through my body as she continued..."They have to do surgery and they don't think he's going to make it." she said crying. I quickly stood up, threw a couple hundred dollar bills on the table and took Monique by the hand and walked her to the door. As soon as the valet driver pulled up I walked her to the passenger side as I pulled out a tip to give him. I got in the car and stabbed off. I must have been doing at least seventy miles per hour in a forty five mile zone. I'm surprised j didn't get pulled over. We pulled up in front of

the hospital. Monique and I both jumped out of the car. I tossed my keys to the valet guy and caught up with her in the ER waiting room...

"What'd they say?" I asked . Monique turned toward me and web open arms. I embraced her...

"They said he's still in surgery and that the doctor should be out here shortly to speak with me." she said scared. I held her tighter as she planted her head against my chest. I walked her over to a pair of chairs and sat her down holding her hand as we waited. As we waited thoughts of who might have done this kept playing through my head, and the it hit me...but before I could further entertain the thought a doctor came into the waiting room. Monique and I quickly rose to our feet...

"Doctor is my brother alright?" Monique asked hurriedly. The doctor seemed to have come
baring both good and bad news...

"You must be his sister Monique—" the doctor said. She quickly responded...

"Yes, doctor how is my brother?" she asked again...

"Your brother is alive. He sustained three gunshots to the abdomen, one to his left arm, and he seems to have taken a pretty good beaten—" the doctor was saying when Monique anxiously interrupted...

"Can I see him?" she asked. The doctor stepped in a little closer to speak to us...

"You can see him...but unfortunately James is in a coma—" he said. Monique almost fell to the floor and burst into tears. Instead I glided her to my chest as the doctor continued..."We were able to pull out all of the bullet fragments and stitch him up real good, but by the time he had got to us he had almost died. We had to sedate him because he was going into shock. Him slipping into that coma mid surgery may have made the difference in saving his life." he said softly.

Monique lifted her head from my chest and wiped the tears from her eyes as she struggled to speak...

"How long?" was all she could muster up...

"The good thing is, over the years of my practice I don't see this being a long term coma. I feel confident in saying that once James's body starts to heal itself, should come right out of it. Until then he will be moved from ICU up to the 24 hour care where myself and my staff will monitoring his progress. As of right now he is still in ICU so if you would like to see him I'll be glad to escort you two back there." he said...

"Yes please, we would really appreciate that." I said relieving Monique of the worry of speaking as she looked too distraught to assemble the words. The doctor walked us to the back where Bossman was. He laid there motionless with IV's lugged into him and a breathing mask over his mouth and nose. Monique rushed over to his side. It angered me to see her so broken, and to see my best friend laying there close to death. I refused to stand there and feel helpless. I

walked out of the room heading for the hospital exit. I knew who had done this and I was determined to make them pay. I didn't get that far away from Bossman's room before I felt a yank on my arm that stopped me in my tracks...

"NO!" she said to me...

"Monique I'll be back." I said calmly. She stepped in front of me...

"No! L.A. look at me—" she said. I kept my eyes on that exit sign until she spoke again. "Frank, look at me—" My eyes connected with hers and she placed her hands on my cheeks as she continued..."No..I know exactly what's going on in your head, and I am asking, no I am begging you not to do it and not to leave me. I just almost lost my brother tonight, and I'll be damned if I allow you to leave and something happens to you. My brother needs you here...L.A. I need you here." she cried. Her tearful plea for me to stay diluted the ball of rage and anger that had manifested...

"I'm not going anywhere. I'm going to stay right here with you." I said. I wrapped my arms around her as we walked back to Bossman's room.

K.I.M.

Men

Fellas...You know, we always say "Real recognize Real" right?...Good, well I can eliminate all of the bullshit because if you made it this far in my book I deem you to be real enough to realize your mistakes and know exactly where I'm coming from when I say...This needs to STOP! Regardless of whether you grew up with your mother in your life or not, we were taught to respect women like you would expect a man to respect you mother, sister, or aunt. But somewhere along the line my brothers have become lost, downgrading from real men that respects a woman the way she should be respected, to these barbaric animals that treat a new pair of shoes, rollie, or some buffs better then they treat a woman. It used to be "Alongside every great woman, there is a great man that loves, respects, and treasures her.". Now its more like "In front of every great woman, there's a brick wall with burn marks and bullet holes from the pain a no good man caused her.". Fellas I know its not easy to say or admit that you have been hurt, Most of the time that's the reason why men are dogs now, because when they tried to love a woman his heart got broken...Guess what....It happens, its life, but what you don't do is allow that hurt to build a barricade around your heart that becomes so cold that you no longer give two fucks about how you treat a woman. It crazy that most of the time we mistreat and misuse the "Good Ones" breaking them into little pieces. Now fellas I'm not saying gibe up your lifestyle or quit being a thug. What I am saying to you is respect our women. Love, guide, and care for them with an open heart, because just like deep down inside of that ice box you call a heart, you have the urge, the desire to be loved. Our women just want that same satisfaction.

Remember, there's a difference between Royalty and a Trap Queen. A real man wants Royalty by his side to help build his empire, there through thick and thin. The boys can play with those Trap Queens.

The Truths Hurts...

It's been a little over a week now and Bossman has yet to pull out of the coma. Monique and I have been spending a lot more time together just trying to keep each other level headed. You could even say we have created a routine. Everyday for the past week or so Monique and I would hang out during the day, go to lunch, or catch a movie, sometimes we would even go bowling. But at night we both would spend the night at the hospital waiting for Bossman to open his eyes. Tuesday morning rolled around and just like any other day I left the hospital to go home, shower, change, and return so that Monique can go home and do the same, but this morning was different. On my way out of the shower I received a phone call from Monique. Her voice was filled with rejoice as she spoke...

"L.A...honey he's awake." Monique said happily...

"I'm on my way." I said. I hopped out and tossed on a jogging fit as I swiftly made my way out of the door. I get up to the hospital as quickly as I could. By the time I made it to the hospital and up to Bossman's room. Monique was standing outside the door and two men were in the room with Bossman...

"What's going on?...What you doing out here?" I asked Monique. Monique folded her arms across her chest and leaned up against the wall as she spoke...

"Ten minutes after James opened his eyes these two Homicide Detectives came barging in. They cuffed him to the bed and told me I had to wait out here until they were done." she said...

"Done with what?" I asked...

"With questioning I guess." she said. The men spent about another ten minutes in the room with Bossman. It couldn't have been going too bad because they uncuffed him and offered a smile as they exited the room...

"Excuse me Detective, what exactly was that all about?" I asked in a tone that more so demanded an answer rather then requesting one...

"I'm Homicide Detective Clay, and this is my partner Detective Marshall. It looks like Mr. James was involved in a random drive by shooting by a group of young thugs." the detective said. Monique interrupted...

"So you have the lowlifes that shot my brother?" she asked. Detective Clay offered a response...

"Yes, and no." he said. Both Monique and I had this confused look on our faces as he continued..."We know exactly who shot your brother. They died about a mile away from where your brothers body was found. From what witnesses and your brother told us, this group of want to be thugs approached him at a party and began to antagonize him with vulgar words of harming him. The thugs approached him and they exchanged a few blows before the other *people at the party broke it up. The wannabe thugs left, and after all of the confusion died down Mr. James departed from the party as well. Witnesses as well as Mr. James verified that once he left the house and headed down the street to his car the thugs pulled up in a black four door Sedan beside him and started shooting at him. When we investigated the scene we found an AK, 45, and 22 bullet casings. Mr. James admitted to us that once he feared his life was in danger he then produced his handgun and started shooting back. The shots that Mr. James fired shattered the cranium of the driver and the car went speeding off at a high rate of speed. With the driver dead at the wheel the car ran into a brick wall on a dead end street at about 70 to 75 miles per hour killing the other three individuals in the car." Detective Clay said. Monique let out a gasp trembling as she asked her next question...*

"So what's going to happen to my brother Detective?" she asked. The Detective closed his note pad and placed an arm on Monique's shoulder as he spoke...

"To me it looks like a clean case of self-defense. We are not going to take him in, but we have to hand the case over to the prosecutors. More than likely they will choose not to prosecute him, but worst case scenario if they do choose to prosecute him even though it was self-defense they will probably want a CCW conviction. Like I said though sweetie I don't think they will press the issue once they get all the evidence in front of them." Detective Clay said...

"Thank you officer. Can we go in and see him now?" I asked hoping to soothe Monique with the presence of her brother...

"Yes...yes of course. He was very lucky to make it through that shooting. God was truly on his side." Detective Clay said. Both Detective Clay and Marshall walked off as Monique and I walked into Bossman's room. His voice was more of a whisper when he spoke...

"Hey y'all." Bossman said. Monique rushed over to his side to embrace him with hugs and kisses. Trying to get her off of him he began to protest...

"Sis...sis I'm good...I'm alright." he said. Monique sat upright and hit him in his leg one time before speaking...

"I was worried sick about you...how are you feeling?" she asked. Monique then sat in the chair next to him and held his hand as he spoke...

"I'm fine MoeMoe, you should have seen the other guys." he said. Bossman then turned his attention to me..."How did you know I was here? The last time I talked to you, you left me hanging for a little bitch." Bossman said. Monique punched him in his arm...

"James stop it." Monique said. Bossman gave a quick response...

"Well its true!" he said. I stepped in a little closer and spoke in the most peaceful tone I could...

"Bro listen, you know like I know that no random chick gonna just come between us. The woman that I was with that night was someone very special, near and dear to me, and I couldn't miss out on my one opportunity at real love." I said. Monique looked at me with a smile as I continued..."We family man, no matter what we go through Ima always be here for you." I said...

"Yeah, yeah, yeah...I accept your apology. Did you at least hit it?" he asked...

"Nah." I answered...

"Did you get some top?" he asked...

"Nah." I said...

"Well what the hell did y'all do?" he asked incredulously. I let out a quick laugh as I answered his question...

"We enjoyed each other's company and got to know each other a little better." I said. Bossman cleared his throat before speaking...

"Well I don't see the fun in that at all, but if you had fun that's all that matters." he said. I placed my hand on Bossman's shoulder as I spoke...

"So when were you planning on telling me your sister was back home?" I asked accusingly...

"Aw man I smoke too much. I could have sworn that I told you, maybe I didn't. I should really lay off the weed." he said. We all laughed and continued talking for about another hour. Monique and I had plans this evening to go out to club LA Pure, a nice Italian spot where you can dance and dine. I wasn't sure if she was still up for going , but I knew if she was then I needed to get a few things ready for tonight...

"Hey, uh...I'm getting ready to get out of here man, I got some business to take care of." I said to the both of them. I leaned in to show some love before taking off...

"Alright, I'll holla at you later. Could you swing by tomorrow by yourself, we need to kick it." Bossman said...

"Yeah my baby, not a problem. I'll holla at you tomorrow." I said. I turned my attention to Monique..."You and Shonda still going out tonight?" I asked her. At first she had this puzzled look on her face, and then it hit her that I was referring to our date tonight...

"Yeah, we still going out. Why what's up?" she asked. Without Bossman noticing, I winked at Monique...

"Oh okay, well let her know I said hey and to call me when she gets the chance." I said. Surprisingly, she winked back...

"I'll be sure to deliver that message." she said. We all again said our peace and I departed from the room. Now already I was late getting started, I still had to pick up a few things and make a few last minute payments. Later on that night I gave Monique a call...

"Hey beautiful how are you?" I asked. I could already tell by the way of her tone as she spoke she wasn't happy...

"You're late...I thought our reservations started thirty minutes ago?" she said a little angered...

"They did, but I already called ahead and informed them that we are still coming." I assured her. She was quick on the rebuttal...

"That still doesn't change the fact that you're late." she said stiffly...

"Well I'm here now, are you ready?" I asked. I know she felt the urge to hurt me through the phone for even asking such a silly question...

"I've been ready L.A...I'm on my way out." she said. As soon as we hung up the phone I saw the door open and her eyes widened when she looked my way...

"Oh...My...God...Is that—" she said surprised. She was stuck. She couldn't believe her eyes...

"Yes its two beautiful stallions strapped to an elegant carriage." I said matter of fact. She slowly walked over to the beautiful beast and gently rubbed their heads, completely mesmerized by the tamed horses..."This is why I was late." I said with a smile on my face. She turned her attention to me with tears ready to run down her cheeks...

"L.A....you really didn't have to do this." she said. I stepped in closer and wrapped my arms around her waist as she continued petting the horses...

"I know I didn't have to, but I did it because I wanted to. I remember you telling me when we was kids that you always wanted that fairy tale moment where Romeo picks you up in a horse drawn carriage. Well, wanting to be treated like a queen is not a fairy tale, not anymore anyway. You are truly something special and you deserve to be treated as such, and I'm not just talking about a temporary feeling. I'm talking about a feeling that will last a lifetime. Rather than just telling you that you are a queen, I plan to continue showing you—" I was saying as I spun her around to face me and I guided her to the steps to climb into the carriage..."My Queen...Your carriage awaits." I said. wiping tears of joy from her eyes she climbed in the carriage and was yet again shocked by the rose petals all over the seats and floor with six dozen flowers that took up almost one corner of the carriage. When I climbed in we were off...

"You have had a very busy day I see." she said as she lifted a rose to her nose and embraced the fragrance...

"Yeah, pretty busy...but it was all worth it to see that big smile on your face." I said. We finally made it to the club and the decor was just as elegant as the name. It wasn't crowded which made it even better and being in a setting where it was mandatory to have formal attire to get in made the experience 10x's more enjoyable. We made our way over to one of the booths against the wall and moments later a man comes to the table...

"Hello, my name is Travis and I will be your waiter this evening. Can I start you off with some drinks?" the Waiter asked. I looked at Monique looking to get an answer out of but her eyes and mind was focused on the beautiful atmosphere...

"Yes, we'll have a bottle of your finest wine." I said. The waiter paused before writing...

"Are you sure sir, those bottles start at about 3,500 dollars." he asked. Monique quickly snapped out of her trans when she heard that...

"3,500!" she said incredulously...

"With all due respect brotha, your job is to be a waiter...which means you wait for the customer to tell you what exactly it is that they want, and you get it. Therefore if I wanted a price check on something I would have asked a cashier." I said seriously. The tall slim built man just bit his tongue and offered a polite response...

"Yes sir, a bottle of wine coming right up. I'll be back shortly to take your order." the waiter said. Monique placed her hands over her lips letting out a little snicker...

"You sure told him." she said in a joking manner before continuing..."Really though L.A., a three dollar glass of wine would have been fine. You really didn't have to spoil me like this." she said. I leaned forward and placed my hand on her chin as I spoke...

"Listen sweetheart, I don't ever want you to think I treat you this way to try and buy your love, because that's not the case at all. I do it for

two reasons. One, because I genuinely want to, and two, because you actually deserve it." I said. She was so lost for words she did nothing but smile, and the waiter returned...

"Are you guys all set to order?" he asked. I handed the waiter the menus...

"Actually we are. I'll have the Chicken Alfredo, and for the beautiful lady, she'll have the Seafood Lasagna with a side of Mozzarella sticks." I said. The waiter finished jotting that down then placed his pen and pad in the bottom left pocket of his apron and began to pour Monique and I a glass of wine...

"If that's all, I will go and put in your order and your food will be up momentarily" he said. I stood up in front of Monique and held out my hand...

"Would you like to dance?" I asked...

"I would love to." she said placing her hand inside of mine as I led her over to the dance floor. A slow song came on, the type you could easily ballroom to, and even though neither of us knew what the lyrics were, we knew how to follow the rhythm of the beat. We start dancing at more of an up tempo pace, and as the music regressed so did our tempo. The last song that we dance to reminded me of "Pretty Brown Eyes" the way it started off. I pulled Monique in closer, body to body. She wrapped her arms around my neck as I wrapped my arms around her waist. We looked into each other's eyes and in that moment everything seemed right, and even though the music was loud it grew mute at the sound of her voice. I could hear her clear as day, our lips literally inches from each other as she spoke...

"Why?...Why jump through all these hoops for me?" she asked in a whisper. brought my left hand up to her chin caressing her cheek with my thumb as I spoke...

"Because...I love you Monique." I said intently. With my hand placed on her chin I guided her lips to mine. Sparks started flying everywhere, and the only thing that was going through my mind

was that I couldn't believe this was actually happening. Here I am standing here with the woman of my dreams who I just told "I love you" and sealed the deal with our first kiss. That kiss lasted every bit of two minutes, and when our lips separated and our eyes opened it was like a

new desire had been awakened in both of us...

"L.A....I love you too." she said breathlessly. We made our way back over to the table where our food had just been placed and indulged in deeper conversation. By the time we knew it the club was closing and the night was wearing thin. We took the longer route back to her place, and the closer we got the more dreadful the thought of this night having to come to an end became. The carriage came to a stop...

"Well I guess this is it." I said as I helped Monique out of the carriage...

"Yup, home sweet home...You know it's kinda late, you could crash here for the night if you want." she said. Even though I already knew Monique wasn't that type of girl I didn't want to risk enticing her or myself...

"Thanks for the offer sweetie, but no...I'll text you when I make it in though." I said. She stepped

in closer to give me a hug and a kiss...

"Alright then, be safe...and don't forget to text me." she said. I watched as Monique walked into the house and locked up before leaving. The next morning I woke up around noon to a text from Monique that read "Good morning handsome, love you" so I responded back. I hopped in the shower then I made my way up to the hospital. It was a beautiful day, and I had a great start. With nothing on my agenda, Bossman caught me on a pretty good day to want to kick it. Before I walked inside of his room I could hear him on the phone with someone...

"No, I just can't work for you anymore. This near death experience made me realize that life is too short, and I don't want to waste it being a drug dealer...I don't need any time to think about it...Then do

what you have to do." he said. The conversation ended with the slam of the phone as I walked in...

"What's up man, everything alright?" I asked. Bossman sat up to speak...

"Everything's good. That was just Duce...I told him I quit." he said. I stepped in and closed the door behind me...

"Bossman you know damn well there's no just quitting when it comes to Duce. Why would you even set yourself up like that?" I asked. Bossman sat in silence for a moment. His voice began to shake as he finally spoke..."I can't continue living with these lies." he said. At first I thought maybe he found out Duce was his father until he continued to speak..."L.A....I know who killed your father." he said as he looked at me with pain in his eyes. His words were like daggers being driven through my heart. I couldn't believe what he had just said. And just like that, my life had been turned upside down, again...

K.I.M.

Women
Ladies I understand that finding a good man is not the easiest task in the world, especially in this day and time. Times have changed, the breed of men has changed somewhere along the line. That does not mean that there isn't any good men out there still roaming. But before you go off blaming the men for their player ways and cold hearts, understand that the way a man treats you and the level of respect a man has for you is reflected through the way you carry yourself. A lot of men feel like "Shit if she don't respect herself, why should I respect her?". And as wrong as it is for a man to have that mindset, its true. Think about it, you end up in relationship after relationship and you either end up hurt or just disappointed and misused. And that commonly stems from you thinking with that fire burning between your legs rather than thinking with your
head. Because if you really stop to think you would see that clearly the perception in which you are putting out is only attracting guys that just want to leave their kids dancing all over your playground. Now your perception may or may not be purposely put out there in that manner. Regardless, it's something that needs to change if you want a man to love you, to truly love you. Only a real man wants a woman of great virtue, a woman that has respect for herself, dignity, ambition, goals, and most of all someone worth investing their time into and open up to. Remember, before you go off saying "Girl ain't no good men out here." take a step back, look in the mirror and adjust your perception, because a man wants a woman worth holding up on a pedestal, and you should put yourself out there knowing you're worthy of being put on one...

Bossman's Story...

Growing up without knowing who my father was, was hard, but to grow up with a single mother trying to take care of two children was even harder. I remember cold nights sleeping together bundled up to keep warm because there was no heat. Watching my mother starve and go hungry just to make sure my sister and I ate. No one understood my story, no one understood my pain, and no one ever gave me anything. I was determined to never have to live like that again, and I remember my first steps I took to make that desire a reality. It was about 17 years ago, my mom got laid off from her job, and bills needed to be paid. Too young to get a job I turned to the streets. I started off with this cat I was going to school with who had already been plugged in and he was letting me work for him selling *little nickel and dime bags. I was only 13 years old when I was forced to give up my childhood, and become a man. Everyday that I wasn't in school I was posted on the corner somewhere making sales. It felt good being able to sneak money into my mothers purse so that she could pay the bills and take care of my little sister. And even though my mother begged me over and over again to leave the streets alone, before I knew it I was too deep in the game to stop. I stopped rolling for Matt after he got locked up in the Fed joint doing 30 to 85 for kidnapping, torture, and murdering one of his workers that ran off with some of his money.*

I was 14 years old when Matt introduced me to his plug, a guy that goes by the name of Duce. He started off reluctant at the thought of me working for him, but after he made a few phone calls to verify my credibility, he hired me. I immediately started to experience the transparent difference between working for someone small and working with the kingpin himself. I went from walking and catching the bus to driving around with no license in my Monte Carlo, with no issue from the police because Duce had them in his pocket as well. I started looking at Duce as a role model after he took me in and basically embraced me as if I was his son. Even though Duce took a liking to me that still didn't change the fact that he didn't play about his money. There was not a pinch of work moving in the city without going through him. The last guy that tried to go around him ended up dead...I know because I was there. It was about a year into me working for Duce when he invited me out to one of his summer parties. He had a huge home so he would throw a summer party there at least twice throughout the summer. The party was jumping with beautiful ladies running around in their two-piece swimsuits and live music. Even though I was by far the youngest one at the party I blended in perfectly. I looked around and there was no sign of Duce, and it was unlike him to not be seen. I went to check on him and see if he was in his office, which he was, but as I approached the door I couldn't help but to overhear a confrontation over the phone...

"Come on now Bigs, everybody has a price....Well I don't see how when I'm offering you the opportunity of a lifetime....Well I'm going to put it to you real plain and simple, you can either get down with the program or you can lay down....You choose your battle, because you know I have no issue with choosing for you....Bigs, I really wish it didn't have to be this way, and you could have just seen things my way." Duce said. I was startled by the rate of speed in which the door swung open. Stuck and speechless I couldn't help but to offer silence in hopes that he wouldn't ask what was I doing kneeled down with my ear to the door of his office. Instead he offered a completely different question..."So, I see you like to eavesdrop?" he said. Even though that was exactly what I was doing I still shook my head in denial...

"No sir, I heard confrontation on my way to the restroom and I didn't see any of your guards, so I figured I would keep guard just in case things got ugly and you needed some help." I said. Duce blatantly

laughed out loud at the ridiculous response, then when he was able to catch his breath he spoke...

"Are you always that quick on your feet?" he asked. I quickly came to the conclusion that my cover was blown, so I simply responded...

"No." I said. Duce gestured for me to step into his office with just a wave of his hand, then he pushed a button on the side corner of his desk and within seconds four of his guards were standing in the doorway with AK-47's in their hands locked and loaded...

"T-bone." he called out to the group of men...

"Yes sir." a six foot seven inch dark skinned man dressed in all black said as he stepped forward. When he stood beside me the only thing I kept thinking to myself was, "damn he big." He had to be about 320, one of his arms weighed more than me...

"I need you to shut down the party, and have a set of wheels ready in ten minutes." Duce said. Without any hesitation the giant responded...

"Yes sir." T-bone replied. Before T-bone and his crew were able to leave the room Duce ordered one last request...

"You know what, make it two sets of wheels. We gotta pay Bigs a visit." Duce said...

"Right away sir." T-bone said as he and his flock left...

"Since you're so good with keeping a lookout I got a job for you young buck." Duce said. Duce placed his hand on my shoulder as we walked from his office, down the back staircase, and into his kitchen...

"What is it?" I asked. He threw on his jacket unwilling to just spit out my task...

"I'll tell you when the time comes...unless you not down with making some easy money." Duce said. If there was one thing Duce knew how to do, it was entice me with my love for money...

"Yeah, I'm down." I said without thinking, and I'm not sure what I just got myself into. T-bone walked into the kitchen...

"The cars are ready and the house was clear of all guests boss." T-bone said. Duce turned his attention back to me...

"Let's go." he said while motioning his arms forward for me to lead the way. We pulled up in front of a house that I later found out belonged to Big's, and we sat there. Duce pulled out his phone and dialed a number. There was a moment of silence and then someone answered..."Hey sweetie how you doing?...That's good, that's good...Hey by any chance do you know where ya hubby at?...Oh, okay he's at Sal's,...Okay well let him know Duce called...Alright sweetie, thank you...You too." Duce said. Duce hung up the phone and patted his driver on the shoulder as he spoke..."Swing by Sal's place." he said. The driver went about two blocks up the street and made a left. The building we pulled up to was a popular nightclub K.O.D., but I assumed it wasn't a regular business day because it wasn't jumping as usual..."When you go in they're going to tell you to leave. Show them this." he said to me as he pulled out a silver card that only had the name Duce on it and handed it to me. "Show them this card and you should have no issues. I want you to go into the back room, unseen and unheard, and keep your eyes out for a man with his kid. Once you see them come back and let me know if they are or aren't there and how many others are in the room." he said. The task sounded easy enough, so I got out of the car and walked into the establishment...

"Hey...Hey kid, what are you doing, you can't be in here!" a voice yelled out. The man was dressed in all black and looked like he could pull a tow truck , so I assumed he was a bouncer...

"Duce sent me." I explained as I showed him the silver card. The muscular man shook at the sight of Duce's name on the card..."Where is your back room?" I continued. The nervous bouncer pointed in the direction of the back room, then he proceeded on. I worked my way to the back room and the closer I got to the set of double doors the louder the sound of men chanting got. I push through the double doors only to see a group of men facing the wall in a half circle. "That must be

Bigs" I thought to myself. He stood out because to his right kneeling right beside him was a child that he was communicating with. The child couldn't have been no older then ten years old. As I turn to leave I catch a glimpse of a few stacks of money in front of the boy. Pretty sure of myself that I was unseen and unheard I quickly made my way back to the car to Duce..."Yeah, he's in there...its like five other people in the room with him. They are all shooting dice." I said. I failed to mention the kid that was there unsure of what was to come next...

"Good." Duce said as he exited the car. I got back out with him as did five out of the eight bodyguards he had with him. As I looked back I noticed that one guard had stood post at the front door...

"Can I help you sir?" a different bouncer called out. This guy was way more polite than the muscle head earlier...

"Yes, get me your manager Tony." Duce said. A the bouncer shook his head...

"I'm sorry, Mr. Tony is not expecting visitors." the bouncer responded. The bouncer pointed his fingers toward the same door we just came in as he continued..."So if you gentlemen don't mind." the bouncer said. Duce nodded his head at T-bone and in that same second T-bone pulled out a Smith and Weston standard issue 45 and cupped it right under the chin of the bouncer...

"I don't want to kill you, but I will" Duce stated, then continued..."Now, let's start over. Go and tell your boss that Duce is here to see him." Duce said portentously. The now shaken up bouncer began to nod his head in acceptance to the request, and ran to deliver the message. Moments later a man emerged from his office space...

"Duce, do you know you have a hell of a way to make an entry." Sal said. The two shook hands...

"Yeah well you know desperate times call for desperate measures." Duce said. The man was about 6'2" and weighed about a buck seventy wet. You could tell he was from the streets, he just dress nice...

"Yeah, listen man, speaking of desperate times. I know I'm late but give me until next week and I'll have all your money." Sal said. Duce began to laugh...

"Sal, Sal, Sal...you always did think everything was about you—" Duce said...

"So what or who is this about then?" Sal asked rudely interrupting Duce...

"Need not you worry your little head about the who's and the what's. What you should worry about is how does me being here tonight benefit you." Duce said...

"Benefit me?" Sal mumbled...

"Yeah, benefit you. See Sal, something or someone that I want is in your club, and you know me Sal, if I want something either I take it or I negotiate. And right now I am in a negotiating mood. So Sal please don't turn me into a terrorist, I'm willing to make you the deal of a lifetime." Duce said. Sal adjusted his glasses...

"I'm listening." Sal said. Duce continued...

"Waiting right inside that door I have a suitcase containing 500,000 cash, and all you have to do is shut off all the cameras, bring me the surveillance tapes for this evening up to this point, you and your workers leave and forget that we were even here." Duce said. I stood there and watched as Sal pondered the offer on the table. A few moments of silence swept the room before Sal finally spoke.

" You know what Duce, after weighing my options here I see I really don't have much of a choice" Sal said.

" Sal, you're a very smart man.... I couldn't have said it more perfectly.." Duce responded with a slight grin on his face, Sal took off to his office to shut down the security system and grab the tape and when he returns so do his men. Duce and Sal shake hands once more as Sal and his bouncers begin to leave...." It was a pleasure doing business with you Sal...." Duce added.

"Yeah...., some pleasure...." Sal sarcastically said, but before Sal could fully make it out the door he was stopped by the sound of Duce's voice. "I'll have T-Bone swing by your house later tonight to drop off an extra 10,000.... That should cover any damages" Duce said. Sal looked as if he may have wanted to say something but he just bit his tongue and proceeded out of the door. Duce, three of his bodyguards and myself moved forward while the fourth bodyguard stood watch at the double doors leading into the room where the men were gambling. Once in the room everything happened so fast yet so slow, it played out slow enough to see it come yet it was too fast to stop anything from happening. The first thing I noticed was the music playing and Bigs and the kid was singing, when they got done Bigs told the kid to blow on the dice. Duce pulled out his snub nose 3-57 and took aim at the back of Bigs head. It wasn't until I overheard Bigs tell the kid "I love you" that I realized the kid was Bigs son. Duce pulled the trigger blowing Bigs brains out, the three bodyguards then opened up fire on the other men.

"Bring it in..." T-Bone ordered over the walkie, I was shocked at what I just saw and was clueless to what "it" was that T-Bone was referring too. Meanwhile the three men started collecting all the bricks of money just laying amongst the dead bodies. I saw the boy mourning over his father's dead body, then my attention was snatched away by the bodyguard bringing in about seven gallons of gasoline and the four of them poured it everywhere. When I turned my attention back to the kid I see Duce walking over to him with a stack of money then tossed it at him.

"All's fair in love and war.." Duce said as he signaled T-Bone to light the room up. The four bodyguards, Duce and myself made our way out of the building and as I looked back the flames had engulfed the door way. It wasn't the doorway of Sal's anymore it was the gates of hell...."You did good son..... you acted on some real Bossman shit" Duce added, and from that day on that name "Bossman" carried

with me. Duce handed me five stacks that were wrapped in thousand dollar increments... "I trust that you will keep this little secret to our discretion..?" Duce asked. Still baffled by the horrendous thoughts going through my head of that boy cradled next to his fathers dead body, yet I still nodded my head in acceptance to Duce's question. When he dropped me off at home I went straight to the shower and sat there letting the hot water hit me. Scared to close my eyes because each time I closed them clips of Duce shooting Bigs in the back of his head, and Bigs brains splattered all over the wall in front of him kept popping up; watching as the boy repeatedly begged his father not to die and not to go is what really took the cake. For days I couldn't eat or sleep, and I was too terrified of what Duce would do or have done to me so I couldn't talk to anyone about what I was going through. A month went pass, then another before suppressing the thought and those images that I had in my head became less painful. Unfortunately that meant suppressing my feelings and emotions as well and as a result I quickly started becoming a negative product of my environment. I started really living that "Dope Boy" lifestyle and allowed myself to be stuck in the ghetto with no inspiration or motivation other than fast money, I knew it would just be a matter of time before I either ended up dead or in jail. That was until I met this kid named Frank but he went by L.A., L.A. was about twelve when I first seen him and his mother was moving into the Oxford apartments just down the hall from my family and I. He and his mother were good people they rarely caused any problems, and as I watched the boy get older I noticed that something about him was different. I figured that with there being no male in the house that the little nigga would be lost and act out in search of guidance, but that wasn't the case with L.A.. I didn't figure out what it was until a few years later when our paths crossed in the most unfair manner. It was a few years after he and his mom had moved in so he had to have been fourteen or fifteen at the time, I remember it like it was yesterday. I was on my way home from making a sell walking down a side street when all of a sudden I hear some commotion, and as I approached the corner I looked to my left and I see two guys that both wore masks but only one had a gun. It was L.A. that the two masked men were robbing and I'm not sure what it was but something told me to intervene. This was the hood, this type of shit happens everyday, I kept telling myself because any other time I would have just continued home but I didn't. I pulled out my 3-57 that Duce had given me and shot in the direction of all three of them. L.A. hit the floor then the two masked men looked back and after I fired another shot they both took off running. L.A. was laying face down on the ground motionless when I ran over I feared that I may have hit him with that first round, then I saw movement from his hand.

"Are you good?" I asked as I kneeled down beside him to help him up. "Yeah, yeah I'm good, thanks for stepping in..." L.A. said as I helped him to his feet.

"I had to man.... its not safe out here" I replied. After that day L.A. and I started hanging out and getting to know each other more. At first I still couldn't figure out what it was about him that stuck out to me, but after a few months I soon found out. I was on my way into the building one day and I saw L.A. sitting on the steps with this look of disappointment on his face, holding a pink slip.... " L.A., what's up man, why the long face...?" I asked but L.A. didn't speak, he just handed me the pink slip...."What's this..?" I asked before opening it.

"Its an eviction notice -" He answered as his voice filled with anger as he continued... "I'm so sick of this shit man... My life has been going down the drain ever since my pops got killed..." He started to say as I interrupted hoping to comfort him with a polite gesture.

"L.A. listen, if its money you need then here...." I said as I reached into my pocket and pulled out all the money I had in that one pocket and tried to hand it to him.

"I don't need your money Bossman, I need to get out of here and make my own..., I need to get my mother out of this hell hole..... I ..... I need you to put me on man...." he said.

"Nah, L.A. man I really don't want you out here in these streets like that...." I said as I shook my head, and I assume that comment pushed a button that sent rage through his body.

" You're not my father Bossman..!!... I had a father before he was murdered in front of me when I was eight years old.... all over a hoe ass dice game.... I sat there with my father in my arms before I was forced to fight through flames to get out of that building.... if he was still here I wouldn't be here in front of you asking you to put me on.... shit I wouldn't have to...., but he's gone and I have to step up to the plate and be a man.... so you're either going to help me or not..." He angrily said. As L.A. spoke it was like being thrown under a bus and it hit me that the boy whose father Duce killed, was L.A.. How could he have survived I kept asking myself, and all of those clips and memories that I had worked so hard to forget came rushing back.

" Where was ya father murdered if you don't mind me asking.." I asked. L.A. sat back down on the steps seeming unsure if he wanted to truly answer the question.

" My mother tells me it was a entertainment center called Sal's Place -" He answered and my face grew pale as he continued..." The fire that night burned the place down, and they replaced that corner with a police station..." He added. A moment of silence moved through the air I couldn't believe what I was hearing, and before I could gather any words to speak L.A. posed the same question as before..." So are you going to plug me.... or not?" He asked. I could see the hurt on his face as well as hear the anger and frustration in his voice.

" To be honest L.A. man I'm not sure if my plug is looking for more help.... but I definitely will call him, let him know about you and what's going on and I'll holla at you tomorrow... cool?" I replied.

" Yeah cool.." L.A. nodded as he responded. We gave each other some love and went inside, when we got to his door we stopped so that I could give him some words of encouragement.

" Listen regardless to what my plug say, keep ya head up.... Imma help y'all get through this .." I

said. L.A. nodded his head and went inside, I started to feel so much guilt for the part I played that night and the fact that he now has to go through hardships because of me. As soon as I got inside the house I called Duce.

" Bossman, what's going on..?" Duce said.

" Duce listen..... I can't talk over the phone, but we need to meet up ASAP!" I said as I tried to hold back the frustration in my voice.

" Well I'm a little busy today, and my hands are tied up all week so....-" he tried saying with disregard to my eager tone.

" Fuck that.... this is information that I am quite sure important enough to make time for.... its about Sal's Place..." I said interrupting him.

" Where are you now?" Duce asked as his voice changed after regrouping from my abrupt outburst.

" Home.." I answered.

" I'm sending a car to come and get you right now.." He said. The black SUV was in front of my apartment building in less than twenty minutes, the ride to Duce's place seemed to have taken forever and the only thing that kept running through my mind was what will Duce do to L.A. once I tell him. We finally make it to Duce's house and the guards escort me up to Duce's office where he awaited my arrival.

" What is it that you believe is so important that it would cause you to impose on my schedule..?" Duce asked in an aggressive tone.

" The..... the boy....-" I struggled to let the words roll off my tongue.

" What boy!" Duce yelled frustrated with me.

" The boy that was with Bigs that night you killed him..." I said.

" Yeah what about him....?" He questioned as he leaned forward.

" That was Bigs son...." I answered.

" Okay, and your point being...?.... the little brat died in the fire next to his father..." Duce responded with his face all twisted up in frustration.

" He didn't die..." I said and I could feel the words suffocate me as I uttered them. As I spoke I watched as his eyes widen and his jaw tighten.

"What are you telling me?" He asked.

" Bigs son survived that night, he didn't die in those flames beside his father..." I said. Duce stood from his seat and began pacing back and forth.

" And you know this how..?" Duce asked.

" A few years back a boy and his mother moved into my building down the hall from me... The Boy's name is Frank, but he goes by the name L.A..... I had already knew there was something different about him but...-" I answered as I remained seated.

" Get to the point..!" Duce yelled as he slammed his hands down on his desk.

" So anyway today L.A. and his mother got an eviction notice and he asked me to put him on in the drug game.... and when I told him no, he started telling me about how his life wouldn't be so fucked up if his father was still here.... Duce he told me how his father got killed, where his father got killed, and how he had to escape the flames...." I said. Duce just stood there for a moment frustrated with his right hand on his head.

" Does he know who killed his father...?" Duce asked.

" No...... he has no clue..." I replied. My answer seemed to sooth the anger of Duce, but for how long I wasn't sure.

" Good..... your job is to keep it that way... Because eventually he will go searching for the truth but now, since I have a inside man your job will be to distract him.... pretend to be his friend, make him apart of your family so he doesn't feel alone.... I don't care what you have *to do just do it. As a matter of fact let's see how good you are at role playing... Get him on the phone and*

put it on speaker... If a job is what he wants, a job he will get.." Duce said. I pulled out my cell phone and called L.A. the whole time the phone was ringing I knew that this drug game lifestyle wasn't what was best for L.A., but it was the only way to keep him safe.

"Hello...." L.A. answered.

"L.A. what's up man, hey listen I talked to my plug and he's willing to give you a job..-" I explained.

" No shit.... that's what's up.." L.A. happily said. I knew what this lifestyle could lead to and I was hoping L.A. would change his mind.

"L.A. listen.... Before you accept anything I want you to think about the road you're heading down.... because the people in this game don't fuck around, especially my plug Duce...... I'm actually with him right now but before I hand him this phone I want you to think about your choice, think about your mother...." I said. A brief moment of silence filled the phone before L.A.

finally spoke.

"I am thinking about my mother..." He said as I handed the phone to Duce.

"L.A. is it?" Duce asked as if he was unsure.

"Yes, and I'm assuming you're Duce.." L.A. replied.

" Your assumption is correct, your friend Bossman here tells me you need some work.." He said reeling L.A. in.

"Yeah, I do..." L.A. responded.

" You know this is a grown man's game.. you sure you ready to play it..?" Duce asked.

"Yes, I'm ready..." L.A. protested without any hesitation.

" Good I'll have Bossman bring you ya first sack this evening..." Duce said. L.A. thanked him as they hung up and Duce tossed me my phone. He walked over to his glass shelf where a few different bottles of liquor sat, and he poured himself a glass.

" You really expect me to pretend to be his friend just so he won't find out the truth.." I asked. Duce took a sip from his glass then sat it back down.

" That's exactly what I want you to do, that boy holds the information yet lacks the identity of those who killed his father... And as long as he stays blind, deaf, and dumb to the truth then he remains a friend. But as of now he's an enemy... and if you don't learn anything from me learn this, you always keep your friends close but your enemies closer... that's how you survive.." Duce said. For years I carried the weight of this secret on my shoulder, keeping the truth from L.A. and it was a secret I was willing to take to my grave until I came face to face with death. Some assholes that L.A and I got into some beef with decided to catch me out at a house party solo. At the most I figured I would just have endured an ass whooping from them, unfortunately it didn't stop there. The four men waited for me inside their car outside and as I was walking to my car I heard a noise, I heard a noise that sounded like the racking of a gun. I was right, soon after hearing that sound I heard the tires on a car coming up behind me screeching and everyone including the driver was shooting out the window at me. It was only by

the grace of God that I took the shots that I took and was able to pull out my gun and fire off a fatal shot to the side of the drivers head, which sent the car speeding off smashing into a tree. As I laid on the ground near death I closed my eyes and I saw God and he appeared to me in the form of an Asiatic Blackman and he spoke to me.

" My son, in your heart I know you are remorseful for your deeds and the path that you chose to steer your life in.... But your time is not up yet my child... you have one last task.... its not too late to undo your wrongs.." As the voice and the image began to fade away I started to feel the warmth of another person's hands latching onto mine, I opened my eyes and there stood Monique.

" Monique...?" I heard myself say in more of a whisper like tone.

" Oh my God James.... you're awake..-" She said before she rushed to the doorway yelling... "Doctor...... Nurse........ somebody.... he's awake dammit.." Monique added. This was my second chance at life and I knew exactly what I needed to do.

K.I.M.

Choose Carefully

In your lifetime you will have encountered two types of lovers and each love is designed to serve a particular purpose in your life. For ladies those two types of Men/lovers are either a Romeo lover or a Casanova lover. A Romeo lover is a man that knows what he wants and will love, protect, respect and cherish you with all of his heart. This is a man that is ambitious about his goals in life, as well as yours. A man that would give you the world yet make you earn it all at the same time. He's a man that will accept you for who you are, and is always in your corner rather you're right or wrong. This is a man that sees the true and divine value in you and wants to see you grow. It's sad to say that in this day in age finding you a " Romeo lover" is rare, but it's true. They are becoming extinct and ladies it's your fault.." Why... How?" you ask, because you choose to waste your valuable time with Mr. Right-Now, rather than building an empire with Mr. Right. A Casanova lover is a boy that " loves " you not for you, but loves you for what he believes he can milk out of you. " Snakes " are typically what they're called, they use their slick tongue for deception. They take your love that you have for them and misuse it to tear you down. You become so weak minded that you eventually allow yourself to be victimized by this heinous love crime, and when that sad story is all over you will find that the true " Romeo lover"

that you were looking for was in front of you from the start. For the men out there the two women you will come across is a Juliette lover or a Coffee lover. A Juliette lover is to a man as a Romeo lover is to a woman, they share the same characteristics of wanting to uplift you, and help you to rise above the conditions of that which you are in. She is a woman with honor, integrity, respect, and love for herself and you. A woman that will love you unconditionally but won't stand for the bullshit, but those women get misused and abused only for a man to want a "Coffee lover". A Coffee lover is also known as a T.H.O.T., not a woman an unstable creature that would rather identify herself as a Bitch than a Queen. " But I'm not a bitch Ima B.I.T.C.H.(Beautiful Individual that Creates Haters)".. For even trying to rationalize you being anything other than a Queen just K.Y.S.(Kill Ya Self). Fellas a Coffee lover will seduce you or play you, just to get what she wants. Really she doesn't want love, she just wants a good fuck and a nice purse. Remember True love is NOT dead, it's just saturated in disloyalty and lies that roll off the tongues of those venomous snakes.

The Truth Hurts

(continued..)

I stood there paralyzed with multiple thoughts going through my

head so quick I could barely piece together a sentence. I couldn't

believe what Bossman was telling me, I didn't want to believe it.

"So you're telling me that Duce killed my father...?" I asked.
"Yes.." Bossman simply responded.
"And the whole time you knew?" I accusingly asked as I stepped in a
little closer.
"Yes L.A. I knew, and for so long I wanted to tell you... but to keep
you safe I didn't.." He explained. I heard sound floating in the air as
he spoke but the words were just going in one ear and out the other.
"So ..... so this friendship this bond that we built, was all just lies and
bullshit?.." I said with fierce conviction as he sat up in the hospital
bed.
" I won't lie to you L.A. at first it was bullshit just all business...
but then we started building this relationship and I truly started
to see you as a brother to me, and I grew to love you like one as
well.." He said, Bossman's words sounded sincere but my ability to
rationalize what was real and what was lies at the moment had been
compromised by the ball of anger that filled my heart.
"Does Duce know you told me this..?" I asked.
"No, if he knew... we would both be dead.." Bossman answered.

" Good we will keep it that way, and if you truly care for me the way you say you do, you will help me avenge my father's death.." I protested. Bossman just nodded his head in acceptance as I handed him his cell phone from off the feeding table.

"What do you want me to do with this...?" he questioned.

" Call Duce back, let him know that you apologize for the phone call earlier, that was the drugs they got you on talking.... and let him know that if the offer is still on the table you would love to be one of his partners.." I explained.

" He would never allow me back.." Bossman said as he shook his head in disbelief. I placed my hand on his shoulder before I offered a response.

" Trust me.... he will.... put it on speaker.." I said. Bossman dialed Duce and put the phone on speaker.

" Bossman, Bossman, ...Bossman what is it... did you come to your senses or something.." Duce asked as he answered the phone.

" Uhh Duce listen, my bad about that call earlier man, its these meds they got me on... if that partnership is still available I'm down.." Bossman said looking over at me as he spoke with sincerity. A moment of silence crept through the phone.

" I'm glad that you are on board, but I haven't heard anything from ya boy..." Duce said. I gave Bossman the thumbs up to tell Duce I was down.

" I actually just got off the phone with him and he told me he's down as well.." Bossman responded.

" Good.... good, I'm glad to see that we all are on the same page... the deal is in four days, meet me at my house at 6:30pm sharp.." Duce said with enthusiasm.

"Will do.." Bossman simply said.

" Oh.... and Bossman..." Duce called out as his tone changed.

"Yeah" Bossman said.

" If you ever talk to me like that again, I will rip your tongue out and make you eat it... Do we understand each other..?" Duce asked. I saw how hard Bossman swallowed before answering.

" Yes sir..." He said before the phone hung up, and for a moment there was a lot of awkward tension in the room until Monique walked into the room.

" Heeeyyy you -" She said as she rushed over to give Bossman a hug before continuing.." How are you doing?" She asked as she fluffed his pillow.

" I'm good sis.." He said. Monique went to him, then turned her attention towards me but by that time I was gone. I went home and the whole ride there flash backs from that night kept popping into my head. I felt this huge burden that was once lifted from my heart being placed back in its original spot, and each thought held a more crushing blow. It was as if the universe was in tune with my emotions cause every station I turned too was on point with how I felt, station 97.1fm was playing "Dance With My Father" by Luther Vandross, 102.7 FM was playing that new Yo Gotti "

Women Lie Men Lie", 88.1 fm played "Friends" by Hoyden and 95.5 FM went old school as well with " Backstabbers" by the OJ's. I couldn't win for loosing so I just turned the radio off for the duration of my drive home. I pulled into my driveway and just sat there for a moment thinking about what I wanted to do. I was trying not to allow my anger and frustration to get the best of me because if it's anything that these streets taught me, it was never allow your enemy to know what your thinking. I was trapped so deep in my thoughts that I was surprised that I was able to hear my phone ringing.

" Hello..." I answered lifelessly.

" Hey honey.... is everything okay?"... you left the hospital in a bit of a hurry.." Monique said as I snapped back to reality in time to piece together a response.

" Yeah I'm good Baby Girl, I had just noticed the time and I was running a little late for a meeting.." I replied.

" Oh okay.... I thought maybe something was wrong... sooo... are we still on for tonight.." she asked but I was unable to remember anything other than what Bossman had just told me.

" Tonight...?" I countered with a hint of confusion in my voice.

" Yes tonight... me.... you... bowling remember....?" Monique questioned with a hint of disappointment in her voice and just like a bag of bricks, it hit me that we did make plans to go bowling tonight.

" Right... right, right yes my love, we are still on for tonight... eight o'clock right?" I asked and just like that I could tell by the tone of her voice she had cheered up.

" Yep, I'll meet you at your place and we'll go from there.... oh I'll drive, and tonight everything's on m." She happily said.

"Whhhaaat...?" I said jokingly.

" Yeah tonight I want to treat my man, it's the least I can do you do so much for me.." She replied. Hearing her say that brought a smile to my face, and for that moment all of my troubles went away then she continued..."Alright love, I'm not going to hold you up from your meeting... I love you, I'll see you tonight.." She added.

" I love you too.." I responded. We hung up and just like that I was reminded of the pain and emptiness of losing my father and growing up watching my mother struggle. I went in the house took a long shower and laid down, I later woke up to the sound of my door bell. I roll over to check the time and its eight o'five, then I looked at my phone and noticed that I had four missed calls from Monique.

"Damn" I said to myself as I jumped up and made my way to the door, I opened the door and Monique stood there in a pair of tan capris with a white shoulder cut V-neck topped with some Jordan's. It was crazy how she made the most simplest outfit look amazing.

" So do you always answer the door for company.... in your boxers..?" she asked as she snickered.

"Actually no, I was just sleep I'm sorry.... come in while I get dressed, I'll be quick.." I said as I stepped to the side to let Monique in and she slowly grazed her finger across my chest as she entered.

" No, take your time.." she said. I closed the door behind her and hurried to my room and into my walk-in closet. I threw on a nice tan button down Polo shirt with a pair of black Cargo shorts and a pair of white Air Force 1's.

" Turn around.... you look good.." She said. I turned around and there she stood in the doorway of my bedroom before making her way closer to me..." I think you should wear the Ferragamo belt rather than the Gucci.... but other than that I'm ready when you are love..." She added before walking off, so I changed my belt and met her in the kitchen.

"Hey open up that drawer.." I said as I pointed. She walked over to the drawer that I was pointing at and opened it..." which one you wanna drive...?" I asked. Monique picked up a pair of keys from the drawer and we headed to the garage, I wasn't sure what set of keys she picked up and she was determined not to tell me.

" Let's go with the Jeep Commander, since I know that's your favorite one.." she said. We both smiled as we got into the car..." so how did your meeting go honey..?" She questioned.

" It was fine, business as usual..." I said without any hesitation. We continued talking for the duration of the ride, but half of me was there with Monique and the other half was planning how I would avenge my father's death. We pulled up to the bowling alley, I had never been here before so at first I was a little uneasy with my surroundings.

"Monique hey, long time no see..." The guy from behind the counter called out, the guy stood about 5'7 one hundred and thirty three pounds maybe in his early fifties.

" Oh Simon hush its only been what a week, you know James was in the hospital" She said.

" Is he okay...?" Simon asked with a sprinkle of worry on his face.

" Yeah Simon, everything's fine..." Monique answered.

" Good I'm glad to hear that, so who is this young gentleman you've brought along with you..?" Simon questioned.

" Simon this is my man L.A., L.A. this is my good friend Simon..... Simon here is the one who showed me how to bowl.." Monique said as she wrapped her arm around mine introducing the two of us.

" It's a pleasure to meet you..." We seemed to say simultaneously as we shook hands before he turned his attention back on Monique.

" Lane sixteen through twenty three is open.... which one would you like..?" Simon asked.

" We will take nineteen.." she answered after looking up at me assuming I would answer the question for her. Once we were at our lane and done setting up we started playing, we sat there for about two hours just talking laughing and bowling. After a while I noticed myself slipping away, daydreaming about what my life would have been like with my father in it...."

Honey are you okay... you seem a little distant tonight...?" She asked me in the most concerned tone.

" Yeah I'm fine baby..." I quickly answered. Monique sat her ball back down and sat in my lap softly cupping my chin in the palm of her hands.

" Frank I've known you long enough to know when something is on your mind.... baby you know you can talk to me about anything right..?" Monique asked or more so stated. I just nodded my head as she continued... " So honey talk to me, let me inside that wonderful brain of yours..."She added. That was always my issue in relationships I never open up, I never allowed anyone into my heart I guess just afraid of getting hurt but Monique was different though and she knew it. You know how Spiderman has Mary Jane, how Martin has Gina, or how Louise has Lane well just like them Monique brought out the best in me she unlocked doors that I thought I had lost the key to and

all without sex. I had not even noticed it until just now that Monique and I have not been physically intimate, so I thought to myself " She must be the one.." and once I brought that thought into existence I found myself answering her question and dropping my guard.

" Have you ever wondered what your life would have been like if your father was still in it...?" I asked hoping that she could understand my pain, but then again how could she?

" Yeah I use too... but now I think nothing would have changed... And honestly I wouldn't want things to change..." She answered.

" And why is that..?" I questioned. Monique placed one hand on each side of my face then kissed me, when our lips released she looked me in my eyes.

" Because if my life would have been altered even in the slightest way... I never would have met you.... L.A. I know you miss your dad but you have to know that he is right there with you every step of the way.... Your father was a great man, I know this because he helped give birth to an amazing man.." She said as she kissed me on my forehead before going on in like a whisper like tone in my ear..." Let's get out of here.." Monique added and that's exactly what we did, we packed up our equipment and went back to my place. As soon as we get inside the house I closed the door and she pushes me against the door and we began passionately kissing. She slowly starts caressing my body as we are kissing so I grab her hands and ram her back into the wall placing her arms above her head. After I slowly peel her shirt off she started ripping off mine, then I pull her hair just to grab a hold of a good spot on her neck with my teeth. I can feel her heart beat racing as I'm leaving hicky's all over her neck while she's griding all against my body. I pick her up and carry her into the bedroom and slowly laid her across the bed before climbing on top of her. I pin her hands down above her head as I slowly work my tongue from her neck to her chest then I kiss my way down her stomach, and as I get closer to her pussy I can feel her body shift putting and arch in her back. I carefully start

unfastening her pants with my teeth and once I get them off she pulls me back up before rolling over, and now she's on top of me. Monique starts kissing me on my neck, down to my chest and as she works her way lower.

" Stop..." I suddenly said. At first she thought I was playing until I repeated myself..." Baby stop.." I said once more as she climbed back on top of me and sat in my lap.

" What's wrong....?.. Did I do something wrong..?" Monique asked with a hint of confusion on her face.

"No, no, no you didn't do anything wrong... its me.... Monique I want this, trust me I do.... but not like this.." I said.

"What do you mean..?" she questioned with even more confusion.

" Monique you mean the world to me, and you have opened my eyes up to what true love is.... and I just want things to be perfect... you get what I'm saying..?" I countered.

"I do actually... and I think its sweet... even though I want to do some really.... really good things to you... I have to respect that don't I..?" She said with a grin on her face before topping it off with a little sad puppy dog face.

" Yeah unfortunately you do...." I said. She leaned in for a kiss as she reached into my pants and grabbed ahold of my dick.

" All I know is.... it better be worth the wait.." She responded as she kissed me on the cheek before getting up to get dressed.

" Yo, its getting a little late you don't have to leave... you can stay the night if you want." I said.

" And why would I stay.." Monique asked with a smile on her face.

" Because.... I just want to hold you in my arms tonight, and I know you want to be held.." I answered. She looked at me for a moment then accepted my offer.

" Okay... I ain't got nothing better to do tonight so I guess I'll stay.." She said as she walked back over to the bed and tried to get in.

"Wait!" I said as I held my hand out in front of her.

" What..?" She asked.

" My bed has a NO PANTS policy.." I tried saying with conviction before we both smiled.

" I see you don't follow your own policy then.." Monique quickly countered. We both removed our pants and get under the cover and went to sleep, her head felt good pressed against my chest. It was one of those moments that I wish never had to end.

K.I.M.

You Can't Buy Love

True or False statement... "Money makes the world go around?". If you picked "True" then congratulations you are right. Economically money does make the world go round, but can money buy you happiness or love? The answer to that is NO, but seeing as how money bought you this book which hopefully will instill or reiterate the meaning of happiness that lies within true love. REAL love can never be bought, sold or taken away, though some individuals base the merits of their love on materialistic things that "love" is never long lasting. Understand that money nor material things keep a relationship together, and a lot of people seeking love in that form believe that the materialistic things are a down payment on their lay way for love. Those same people seeking love in that manner use the materialistic things as leverage to make the one in which their seeking feel obligated to stay, giving the seeker a sense of ownership or belonging. Then there are people that ONLY seek those who will shower them with those materialistic things only loving them for what he/she can get out of them. These snakes usually target those that are broken, weak and unaware of their worth that they will do whatever it is necessary to keep that person in their life. When the blood suckers are finally gone you end up more damaged than what you started out. Regardless to which side of the field you play one of two things will happen, you either end up financially broke or hurt. Worst case scenario BOTH, you do not belong to anyone nor does anyone truly belong to you its just your turn. "What do you mean..?" I mean it's just your turn to try your best to make an impact on their lives that allows them to see that with you is where they want to be.

Remember that there is always an option to love but NEVER an obligation.

The Final Deal

" Ah.... L.A. man I know you there, pick up the phone man we need to talk.." Bossman said. Bossman had left the same voicemail on my house phone as well as my cell phone three times before finally just popping up at my front door. I have already been up for hours I'm not even sure if I slept the night before. As if the phone wasn't loud enough the sound of my door bell being rung repeatedly snapped me out of my trans.

" Coming" I yelled out as I crawled out of my bed and made my way to the front door. I opened the door and Bossman stormed in all frantic. "I'm not sure about this L.A. , I'm really not sure.." he said as he paced the living room.

" Sure about what?" I asked as I closed the door and attempted to calm him.

" Crossing Duce.... he will have us killed just thinking about putting a hand on him.." Bossman

stated in a very high tone. I placed my hand on his shoulder stopping him from pacing before I sat him down at the kitchen table.

"Listen... our plan is bullet proof, we make this final deal and after its done we tie him up put him in the trunk and leave him there.... You and I split the money and we get as far away from here as possible..." I explained confidently.

" And what about his guards, they just gone sit by and let the shit go down..?" He questioned as I sat down in front of him.

"Bossman we have been over this for the past three days.... all we have to do is convince him that he doesn't need any bodyguards...-" I was saying before I was rudely interrupted.

" And what in the hell makes you think that that he's going to go for that...?" Bossman questioned as his level of anxiety started to rise.

" The key word tonight is TRUST... we play our ""You trust us right?"" card along with our "

We're your new partners.."" card and make it so convincing that he falls for it..." I said as Bossman started shaking his head doubting that the plan will work.

" I don't think I can do this..." he said as he stood up heading for the door to leave but I stayed seated as I spoke words of power and truth.

" You really don't have much of a choice... you can either walk out that door forget this plan and continue living your life in the shadows of Duce, knowing he will never let you go... or you can make a stand today and break the chains from around ya neck that Duce has the key to.... And if not for yourself, do it for my father.... You at least owe him that much to try.." I said causing Bossman to stop at the kitchen doorway with his back facing me.

" I'll do it....-" he mumbled before going on.." I'll do it for you L.A.., I ruined your life or at least played a role in doing so, and I know that words won't bring him back so the least I can do is try to make things right..." he added.

" Thank you man, that really means a lot to me..-" I said as he turned around, I stood up and we both gave each other some love before I went on... "And hey I'm glad that you stopped by...

After all this is done tonight me, you, and Cell should go out and have a few drinks..." I suggested.

" Uhhhh, I don't know.... you know Janel hasn't let me out of her sight since I came home Sunday... the only reason I'm here now is because she had to work.." Bossman explained as he scratched his head.

" Well here's what you do.... what time does she get off..?" I asked as I walked over to the refrigerator and pour me a glass of Minute-Maid.

" About 5:45 pm..." he answered.

" Okay cool its 12:15 now so you have time to think about how you gone do this, okay when she gets home start a huge argument for no reason and just storm out... she'll give you some time to cool off and you can just come over here, I should be back by then.." I said.

"I like the way you think....and where are you going...?" he asked with a grin on his face.

"Well I, my good man, am going to check on my mother and see how she's doing.. its been a while since I've been out there..." I answered as Bossman looked down at his watch.

" Well ain't nobody tell you to move her all the way out there so far away from the city... and its really not that long of a drive just an hour and a half there and the same back.." he said.

" Yeah okay that may not be far for you, and besides I had to get her away from the city.... she's safer there than she would have been in the city, shit you know she's all I got.." I said.

" Yeah L.A. man I understand, well Ima get out of your hair and let you get yourself ready for your little short trip... oh and tell mama I said hey.." he said as I walked him to the front door.

"Alright will do, I'll meet you back here around seven o'clock.." I said.

"Alright little bro... one..." he responded as he stepped onto the porch.

"One.." I replied as I closed the door then went to hit the shower. After I shower and get dressed I hit the road, and midway to my destination my phone rang... "Hey baby I was just

thinking about you.." I said as I answered the phone.

"Mmmhhmm, I'm just sure you were..-" Monique responded in a soft tone jokingly as she continued... "So where are you Mr...?" she asked.

" Well how do you know I'm not at home..?" I asked offering a question to a question sarcastically.

" Well for one I just stopped by your place, and secondly I can hear the engine of your car accelerating... so you want to try again...?" She questioned as she laughed.

" *You went by my house.... so now you're stalking me ..?" I countered once more.*

" *Stalking..... you?" she said laughing again before going on..." No sweetheart I'm not one of your little groupies... I was actually stopping by because I had a surprise for you... and you still have yet to answer my question..." Monique added.*

"*Well if you must know I'm on my way to see my mother, I haven't seen her in a while so I figured I would surprise her... speaking of surprise, I have one for you as well... what's paper thin, easy to get and changes depending on your destination..?" I asked, then a moment of silence filled the phone as I gave her a moment to think.*

" *Currency..." She answered.*

" *Nah your close.... I actually didn't think of that one... No but its tickets... I'm going to stay the night here with my mother but when I get back I have two plane tickets for Thursday morning leaving here going to London.." I said.*

" *Oh..... My....... GOD....! .. really babe? you really didn't have too.." She said as I could hear the excitement in her voice.*

"*Babe I know I didn't have too, I wanted too... you have been working so hard taking care of your mom and your brother shit you deserve a vacation.... and I'm going to make sure you get it.." I said in a soft tone.*

" *OMG .... I am sooo excited.... what all should I bring...?" She asked but little did she know excitement was racing through my body as well.*

" *Pack very light cause I plan on taking you shopping when we get there .... but I'm pulling up to mamas house now so I'll see you tomorrow..." I answered.*

" *okay babe, tell mama I said hey..." she said.*

" *Will do, love you..." I said as I pulled into mamas drive way.*

"*I love you too" She replied. As soon as I stepped out of the car I could smell the beautiful aroma of meatloaf and greens in the air..." That's* mama" I said out loud to myself, I could always tell when mama was cooking. I walked over to the front door and reached underneath the window ledge grabbing the spare key..." Mama... mama.." I called out as I opened the front door.

" Look at you..-" Mama said as she made her way from the kitchen right into my arms, then she gazed into my eyes before going on..." You didn't tell me you was coming..... so what do I owe this visit?" She questioned just grinning from ear to ear.

" Nothing mama, I just figured I would surprise you that's all..." I answered.

" Surprise or not I know my child... come sit.... sit..." She said motioning her arm towards the couch as she continued..." You want some tea or coffee?" she asked.

" No ma I'm fine..." I said as we sat down, she sat up and placed her hands over top of mine.

" What's wrong son... you got that look in your eyes...?" she questioned. My mother and I had a tight bond before my father was murdered and when he died it did nothing but bring her and I that much closer making our bond unbreakable. I can talk to my mother about anything without her being judgmental or getting angry with me.

" I found him..." I said in a shallow tone as I took a deep breath. I watched as her face twisted up.

"Found who..." She dared to ask.

" The man that killed my father..." I said and I felt my mothers hands begin to shake as I went on..." And tonight I'm going to confront him face to face.." I said. I watched as tears in my mother's eyes ran down her cheek only for me to wipe them away.

" L.A. and then what..... why haven't you just called the police..." she said painfully.

" Ma you know that's not how this works, and even if it did.... you know the police wouldn't do a damn thing... listen just know that If *anybody comes asking you where was I tonight, you tell them I was here with you laying on the couch.." I explained.*

"Frank... what are you planning on doing..?" she asked as her face lit up with curiosity and pain.

"Ma, I love you and you know I would do anything for you...-" I tried saying as I leaned in and gave her a kiss on the cheek.

" Then don't do what you're thinking about doing son.... you're all I have..." she said crying as she begged me to stay and rethink what I might do.

"Ma.... I gotta go.." I said as I stood up and made my way to the door, then my mother just dropped to her knees and began to pray.

"Lord God of Israel... please watch over my child, guide him so that his heart won't be so filled with anger, Lord God of Israel I ask that you guide my son home safe and unharmed and that you bring justice to those that have caused him pain... I ask these and all other blessings in the name of the Lord God of Israel... Amen, Amen, Amen.... " she said and I watched as she opened her eyes and looked into mine.

"Amen...... Justice will be brought.." I said as I walked out of the door and made my way to my car, so much pain and frustration flowed throughout my veins as I watched my mother wipe her tears away through her picture window as I backed out. On my way back to the city I made a few stops, one being the mall to holla at my boy Ace.

"Hey.... L.A. how you?" the little old Chinese man said.

"I'm good Ace baby what about you?" I questioned as Ace came from behind the glass to shake my hand.

"I'm good my friend... just fine." Ace answered.

" is that what I think it is...?" I asked as I pointed over at one of the glass showcases. I was actually surprised myself at how beautiful the piece looked.

"Yes... yes it is, it just came in for you yesterday, I was going to keep it in the back but then I saw how beautiful it was .... I just had

to showcase it.. you have very good taste I must say my friend.." he explained as he removed it from the showcase and boxed it up for me. " Thanks again Ace, I know it was last minute but I'm digging it.." I said.

" You loyal customer, like family.... anything for youuuu.." the little old Chinese man said as he waved his hand as if to shoo me then we shook hands before I departed. While already at the mall I stopped over at "Lover's Lane" to pick up a few things to put into my "special bag" for this trip. After leaving the mall I made one last critical stop and the whole ride there I kept thinkin about what my mother said to me. I pulled up to the police station, parked then went inside.

" Can I speak to officer Boyer please?" I asked the lady officer at the front desk.

" And what exactly is it concerning...?" the lady questioned as she looked at me wired.

" It's kinda personal..." I leaned in and said in a soft tone. The lady picked up the phone and punched in a three digit number, she began speaking quietly into the phone before she hung up then turned her attention back towards me.

" Officer Boyer will be right with you.." the lady said.

"L.A?...." A voice called out moments later in more of a question like manner.

" Officer Brandi Boyer... how are you..?" I asked as I turned around. I hope I haven't lost you let me explain... Remember BB from the lock-in party a few years back, well come to find out she was studying in law enforcement back then and that passion grew into reality. Now she's a police officer working as dispatch, we ran into each other at a local strip club about a year ago she was there celebrating her birthday and I was there enjoying my single life. We ended up hooking up that night, I was supposed to call her but I got busy.

"I'm.... good... a little shocked to see you here... what is it that you're doing here if I may ask...?" BB questioned.

" Is there somewhere we could go to talk in private...?" I asked as I noticed the nosy lady at the front desk lean an ear over to eavesdrop. BB checked her watch.

"It's time for me to go to lunch anyway... it's a cafe down the street we could grab some coffee and talk..." she said.

" Yeah that's cool, I only have an hour to spare then I have to get going..." I said after looking down at my watch.

"We've done far more in less time... I'm sure we will be fine.." BB said teasingly as she fixed the collar of my shirt and we both shared a laugh as we walked down the street to the mini cafe. We ordered our coffee at the front desk then took a seat.

"So L.A. what do I owe this pleasure..?" BB asked.

" BB listen I need a favor, one that could possibly cost you your job if anyone was to ever find out.." I said as I scooted in closer to her. She leaned in closer with curiosity and worry in her eyes.

"L.A. if its something that could cost me my job.... then I'm sorry I can't help you.." she said and as she got up to leave I stood up blocking her path.

" BB hear me out, I wouldn't ask you unless I really needed your help..." I pleaded as she sat back down.

"I'm listening.." She said.

" Truth is, there's something going down over on Oxford between Pocket and FivePoints... I have no idea what's going to happen but I need you to be on the look out tonight for any calls to dispatch a unit to that area.... and if a unit does get dispatched there, I need you to send them elsewhere" I explained.

" L.A. if you know something is going down why don't you just alert the police so we can resolve the issue...?" She asked in a loud whisper tone before I sat back in the chair as the waiter brought us our coffee.

" For one I don't fuck with the police..., secondly I'm not a rat and lastly this is a matter in which needs to be carried out the way its intended.. the only thing I'm asking of you is to create a distraction

IF one is necessary.." I replied once the waiter left and after I spoke we both sat in silence as she thought over my request.

"Okay... I'll do it..-" She said as she leaned in closer placing her hand on my knee working her way up... " But what's in it for me..?" she asked. I took her hand off of my inner thigh and placed it back on the table, now true indeed it would be cheaper to just break her off a piece of this summer sausage but I love Monique. Therefore I wasn't doing anything to jeopardize our relationship.

" Twenty thousand dollars.." I said with a cold stare and BB just laughed for a moment thinking that I was joking around.

"Wait.... you're serious aren't you..?" she asked but the blank stare on my face alone should have served as an answer to her question.

" Yes, I'm very serious.... and I have it all right now in cash... and its all yours if you choose to accept.." I responded for clarification as I pulled out a tan envelope and sat it on the table. Moments passed as she looked at me then the envelope, back at me before refocusing her attention on the envelope.

"I'll do it...-" BB said as she grabbed the envelope and put it inside of her purse.

" I'm glad that we were able to do business..." I casually said as I looked down at my watch then continued..." Unfortunately I have to get going, it was a pleasure seeing you again officer..." I added as we both stood up and embraced each other.

" It was nice seeing you as well L.A..." BB said sweetly as we both left the cafe and went our separate ways. I wasn't sure if BB would sell me out or not, then again she has no idea what's going to happen but neither do I for that matter.." My mother might be right.." I said to myself as I walked to my car. I made my way home poured myself a cold glass of peach Amsterdam trying to mellow myself out and listen to my voice of reasoning, but I was interrupted in my thought process by a knock at the door..." Its open.." I shouted then Bossman came right in and into the kitchen where I was..."Damn..... what happened to you..?" I asked after looking at his face, his lip was busted and he had a nice little scratch going down the side of his neck. "Truthfully it looked painful" I thought to myself as he sat down on the stool leaning on the counter top.

"Mann, so I took ya advice right..-" He said.

" I suggested that you get into an argument with her not get into a boxing match with her.." I said as I began to laugh.

"Ha, ha you got jokes... just so you know I did start an argument..... then I called her fat in the dress that she had on.." he explained.

" Ooooooo, why would you do something stupid like that...?" I questioned.

" That was the only thing I could think to say that would make her let me leave.." he answered shaking his head as I reached into the freezer and grabbed him a bag of frozen corn to get the swelling to go down before I started laughing some more.

"Yeah you left alright...it look like ya ass took a two piece and a biscuit with you.... to go..." I jokingly said before he snatched the frozen bag of corn from me.

" Yeah whateva man, its better than what Duce will do to us if he finds out our plans" Bossman said and as much as I hated to admit it Bossman is right, Duce would kill me without hesitation if he knew we were planning on playing him. I do have one advantage though, Bossman doesn't know that Duce is his father therefore Bossman is equally terrified of the consequences. That advantage eases my mind because Bossman will maintain his loyalty to me in hopes of gaining his "Freedom" from Duce.

K.I.M.

Know Your Worth

With this game we play called love you get back what you put yourself out there to be worth or valued as. If you put yourself out there as a person of low value then that's the response you will get from love. If you put yourself out there as a person of high value then a great response you will get. See love always begins with a measurement of self worth, just loving yourself and from there how you carry yourself dictates how most people will treat you. For true love to exist between two people they must both find each other worthy of one another's respect, honesty, loyalty, patience, commitment and time. If you can't see the true divine value in yourself then you don't carry yourself as a man or woman of value so consequently you become mistreated and misused, clearly not given a fair chance at love. You can't easily be worth someone's Time and Respect, but never worth their Honesty. Clearly that's nothing more than a long lasting relationship with respect behind a dark closet of lies. Truthfully you don't deserve that, every man and every woman that deems themselves to be worthy of true love should never settle for anyone not willing to give it to them. With true love comes time, with time comes patience, with patience comes commitment, with commitment comes respect, with respect comes honesty and with honesty comes loyalty. If you feel like you're worthy of these six things then understand that you are worthy of love, true love. Just remember to find yourself and once you find yourself you will know your worth, once you know your worth MAKE IT KNOWN. Closed mouths don't get fed.

Moment of Truth!!

Even though Bossman or myself admitted it we both were very

nervous when we pulled up to his house.

"Listen man, as far as the plan goes just let me do all of the talking.." I said to Bossman as he nodded at me in confirmation. We both got out of the car and made our way to the door and before either of us could knock or ring the door bell, one of Duce's guards opened the door.
"Duce is waiting for you two in his office, follow me" the guard said. The guard walked us up to Duce's office and I saw Duce sitting behind his oakwood desk waving us in to have a seat as he finished his conversation on the phone.
"I know, I know... it's no need to worry, everything is on schedule..... okay I'll see you in about an hour .... okay, bye.." He said as he hung up the phone and turned his attention to Bossman and I ..." Fellas .... what's going on.." He asked and just the grin on his face made me want to beat his ass and leave him for dead right where he sat.
"Nothing much.... you?" Bossman said cutting the unknown tension in the air.
"Well let's see...... I'm getting ready to make one of the biggest deals of my career and then hand the business over to you two..-" he said as he let out a slight laugh before going on.." So I'm feel pretty damn good, and pretty damn old too if you ask me..." he said pausing to motion his hand over towards the bar.." Drinks?" Duce asked.
"Yeah I'll have one..." Bossman quickly responded.

" I'll have one as well.." I said figuring that a drink will help me relax. Duce poured up three medium size glasses about halfway, we all grabbed our glasses and Duce raised his in the air.
" I would like to propose a toast...-" Duce said and Bossman and I raised our glass as Duce continued.." Here's to a new partnership, a family, and most importantly.... money.." He added
as all three of our glasses rang together.
" So who are we making this sell too..?" I asked after taking a sip from my glass but Duce finished his shot before offering a response.
" It's a biker gang that go by the name A.F.H or Angels From Hell.... they're just starting up and they want two hundred and fifty keys of crystal meth... Mostly cash, the rest is eighty thousand in diamonds.." Duce said as Bossman and I looked at each other in shock. I knew I wasn't the brightest candle on the cake but I know that meth was usually $215 a gram which meant that with the money and diamonds combined tonight's deal was a little under fifty three point three million. Bossman and I was stuck for a moment and I just know he was thinking the same thing that crossed my mind, that's almost twenty six point seven million a piece..." Boys.... boys close your mouths before something flies in there.." Duce added as he started to chuckle.
" Ah... Duce that's a lot of money... who all you got coming with us .?." I asked once I was able to gather my thoughts.
" Just us three.." he simply said..." oh that reminds me..." he paused once more as he walked over to his desk and pressed a speaker button that traveled through the house before he went on.." Attention... attention... I need everyone in the kitchen immediately..." he finished. I was still puzzled, did he just say he wasn't bringing anyone with us.
" And why won't your guards be escorting us tonight..? " I stupidly asked.
" Well for one reason and one reason only..... Trust... the leader of their biker gang used to be apart of the Mexican Cartel and he already

knows how I role... In this game L.A. it's hard finding someone you can really trust, but once you find that person... you treat them with a little more respect and dignity than the others.... José Sanchez is one of those people I don't have to bring an army with me to make a deal with and he respects me in that same manner..." Duce said as we made our way to the kitchen and when we got there, there's about twenty five guards and seven maids just standing there.

"What do you think this is about..?" Bossman asked. I motioned to him to silence himself as Duce began to speak.

"Ladies and gentleman I would like for you to turn your attention to the two gentlemen to my left... get a good look at them because once I walk out that front door .... I am no longer your boss.... they are ... I expect that you will treat them with the same respect, dignity, integrity and honor that you would treat me with...-" he walked over and stood between us and placed his hands on our shoulders as he introduced us..." This is Bossman the loyal thunder cat out of the two.... And this is L.A. the mastermind or brains if you will, of the two... these two men have dedicated their lives to the game, and I truly consider them family...... so fellas now that that's out of the way, we should get going.." Duce finished as Bossman and I nodded agreeing simultaneously.

"Yeah, we should...." I said as Duce tossed me a pair of keys.

" Today will be the first of many days you will ride in style my boy.." Duce said.

" After we're done Duce, I have to go and check on my OG... she's in the hospital.." I quickly responded thinking of an exit plan in case shit goes left.

"Not a problem son, I understand its always family first... Bossman will just drive your car behind us and when the deal is done I'll just have him take me to the airport, that way you can handle your business..." Duce replied with what seemed to be genuine compassion.

" Cool" Bossman said.

"Alright, let's role.." Duce suggested. Bossman went out the front door to my car while Duce and I went out the back door.

"Damn...." I said in a whisper like tone as I laid my eyes on a beauty, after admiring it for a moment I spoke..." A 1998 RR, original rims, custom paint with tented windows..... nice.." I said in astonishment.

" I see you know your cars.... she's a beauty isn't she..?... come on let's get going.." Duce said. We got inside the car pulled around to the front where Bossman was waiting and he followed behind us, as we drove off Duce lit a cigar and even though I was hoping he didn't say a word the whole ride, sure as shit he did.

"Is your mother okay..?" Duce asked catching me off guard.

" She'll be fine, she has surgery in the morning and I promised her I would spend the night at the hospital with her... just to be there with her before the surgery.." I answered as I left a suspenseful silence in the air that seemed to help convince Duce of my lie.

"Well ..... my prayers are with her..." he said as he placed his hand on my shoulder before going on..." Make a left at the next light ... " he added and I was completely confused and lost.

"I thought we were going to Mike's Place.." I said. Mike's was a famous local bar and grill it was one of those establishments in the city that lived by the motto "Money talks, bullshit walks.."

which meant if you ain't have that money or your name wasn't ringing any bells in these streets then you wasn't getting pass the front door.

" Yeah we were, but there has been a change of plans.." Duce responded. My heart began to race and the only thing that kept running through my mind was the fact that Bossman just might have sold me out, but then my phone rings and it's him.

"Hello" I answered.

"What's up L.A., what's going on... where are you going..?" Bossman questioned. I felt Duce's eyes burning a hole in the side of my face, so I chose my next few words wisely.

"Its been a change of location... just follow me.." I said before hanging up the phone.

" A bit of a worry box that one...?" Duce asked.

" Nah, he just don't like being left in the dark when it comes to changes... and quite frankly neither do I..." I said as Duce put out his cigar.

" See I knew there was something I liked about you...you remind me so much of myself, so much fire, so much ambition so much leadership potential and I respect that..-" he said pausing for a moment thinking before continuing.." Mr. Sanchez called me right before you and Bossman showed up and insisted on changing the meeting spot because he had just found a mole in his

organization... and he wasn't sure who all the mole told about the meeting tonight... and if anything was to happen he didn't want me thinking that he had set me up. So instead of calling the deal off I agreed to meet him at this abandoned Pepsi warehouse that should be coming up in about half a mile..." Duce explained. My heart rate began to ease once he informed me about the situation.." There it is.... pull in here..." He added as I pulled in pass the gate and went around the building to the loading dock. When I pulled around there was three all black SUV's with limo tent glass parked in front of a silver garage door connected to the warehouse. I parked the car and waited for Bossman to walk up to our car since he parked my car back a nice distance. Once Bossman made it up to Duce and I we got out of the car and I noticed five men armed with Mac-10's standing in the doorway of the now opened garage door. Seconds later two men pull up in front of us on some classic Harley Davison's and the two men were dressed in all black aside from their leather jackets that read " Angels From Hell". Both men got off of their bikes and removed their helmets.

" Capasa Amigo..." The older Latino who looked to be in charge yelled out as he greeted Duce with a firm handshake and quick hug.

" Good to see you again my friend.." Duce said before turning his attention to Bossman and I..." Boys this is Mr. José Sanchez , Sanchez this is Bossman and L.A. my new partners I was telling you about..." Duce said to the man which stood about 5'8, slick hair but no facile hairs and he had to have been no more than a hundred and thirty pounds. Sanchez was one of those guys you can just look at and go " Damn he's had a rough life.".

"No need for formality fellas... you can just call me Sanchez .." he said after acknowledging us with a simple nod. The man spoke as if he had only been in America a few weeks, I mean he spoke good English his accent was just so stern..." And this is my dope head junky of a brother that I was telling you about... we just call him "head" a moment of silence filled the air as Head just nodded acknowledging us before he went on.." Alright enough with all of the introductions, I believe we have some business to attend to." Sanchez added.

" Yeah we do.." Duce said as we walked over to the open garage door. Duce was the only one who dared ask what Bossman and I was thinking..." So Sanchez, what's with all the heavy artillery..?" Duce asked. Sanchez who was already ahead of us turned around while walking backwards offered an answer to the question.

" Trust me, they're more so here for your protection then mine..." Sanchez casually said. As soon as we walked in, the first thing I noticed was this slightly elevated platform in the middle of the room with a table and three heavy duty suitcases with wheels on top of it. There was also a bright light fixture hanging above the table shining down directly on the suitcases, but other than that the place was completely empty. Duce had already signaled two of the armed and assigned help, to retrieve ten briefcases containing the "goods" from the trunk of his car. The men brought
in the briefcases in and sat all but one of them on the floor next too the table, while the last case was placed on the table. Sanchez opened the case and pulled out one of the twenty five bricks that the briefcase

contained and Sanchez simply sat the brick on the table next to the briefcase. Head pulled out his pocket knife and carefully penetrated the plastic with the tip of it, the room grew silent when he took the powdery drug that was caked up on his finger and bring it to his nose and taking a good hit. With his head tilted back and his eyes closed Head began to hum.

"What exactly is he doing..?" Duce questioned before the humming stopped but only momentarily then Head started up again.

"No need to talk in such a low tone, see Head here is deaf.... the poor bastard got into a bike accident a few years back and they had to remove a piece of his brain that was badly damaged... Unfortunately he lost his ability to hear and speak, so him humming is his way of letting me know to either purchase a product or not.. When he hums once that means no..-" Sanchez said.

"So what does two hums mean..?" Duce inquired.

" That my friend, means we have a deal..." Sanchez answered as he grabbed the brick and placed it back inside the briefcase. He snapped his fingers signaling for his men to take the briefcases to the cars before he continued..." Like always Duce, it was a pleasure doing business with you.-" he said pausing as he shook Duce's hand before handing him the sack of

diamonds.." It was also a pleasure meeting you two as well, I look forward to conducting business with you two in the future.." Sanchez said and Bossman and I simply nodded our heads at Sanchez as him, Head and their goons departed. It seemed as if right after the transaction was completed and the biker gang left everything just started moving in slow motion, then Duce turned his attention to Bossman and I before speaking. As he spoke I zoned out and it was like I was in the twilight zone I started having flashbacks of the night my father was killed, and it was as if I was a child all over again just helpless and afraid. I remember my father winning and talking cash *shit and all the men that night were betting big, something like five thousand dollars a roll.*

KANGAROO COURT

It was on my pops to roll the dice so he kneeled down to one knee, and I got right down there with him I guess you could say I was his "Good luck" charm. He rolled seven then eleven before collecting his winnings from those two rolls and handing the pile of money to me. He rolled an eight on his next roll, he stay on the dice for a long time and all the while was killing them on the side bets. A few rolls later my father still had no luck hitting his point so he sat up straight and looked me in my eyes as if somehow he knew this would be the last time he saw me. I remembered him placing his hands on my shoulder and smiled as he fixed his lips to say.

"What you know about this song son..?" he questioned. The question caught me by surprise when he asked it because I was completely unaware that I was even singing to begin with. My father would always glow when he heard me sing which made him always call me his little Lyrical Angel which was where L.A. came from.

"What you mean pops I've heard this song a few times before... you were just always at work when mama and I would be jamming..." I answered. He smiled as we both started singing the chorus of the song together.

"For the love of money.... People will rob their own mutha.... for the love of money...-" We both sang. Smiling at each other he handed me the dice and blew inside my hand telling me to shake them up real good and wish for lucky number eight. That's exactly what I did I tossed the dice up against the wall and for a moment it was like everything went silent, one of the dice stopped on three as I watched the other continue to spin. All of a sudden that soothing silence was broken by an extremely loud bang followed by the stench of smoke. I quickly covered my ears before I looked over to my left and saw my father face down on the floor, his eyes were shimmering at me with

a tearful gloss. As blood was running down the side of his head I crawled over to him, placing my face on the floor directly in front of his I watched as tears ran from his eyes to the floor bord.

" I....... I lo...... I love...-" He mumbled as he struggled to speak but before he could finish his sentence he died.

" No.... no....no.... dad wake up... dad please.." I pleaded as my tears of pain, anger and frustration fumbled to the floor.

" Uh... yo.... what about the kid...?" I heard a voice call out, my heart began to pound as I cradled my father's head in my arms then I heard another voice.

" Leave him.... shid he ain't no threat.." the other voice called out. As they picked up all of the money, the man that told the others to leave me alone grabbed two stacks of money out of a black duffle bag... " Aye..... aye kid..." the man said as he tossed the two stacks in front of me while the other men were dousing the room with gas. The repulsive aroma quickly filled the air and I struggled to catch a glimpse of the man that tossed the money at me. I wiped my eyes hoping that eliminating the tears would improve my vision, but the water flow would not stop...." All's fair in love and war.." The man added, and those was the last words that he said to me before signaling the other men to light the gas. Then all of a sudden I started hearing fingers snapping.

Back To Life Back To Reality...

"Ah.... hello.... L.A. man you good.?" Bossman asked while tapping me on my shoulder bringing me back to reality.

" Yeah.... yeah I'm good.." I responded but truthfully I wasn't, I had a bomb inside of me that was ready to go off at any moment. I never knew that I could feel so much pain, so much rage, anger and hatred towards another human being.

" Fifty three point three million fellas.." Duce said as a grin fell upon his face while he made his way over to where Bossman and I was at before going on..." Other than the beautiful diamonds, today..... today was a beautiful day... I'm going to miss doing business like this with you boys.." he added hesitant to continue.." You boys already know that y'all are like sons to me, sons I never had.." Duce said as he handed me his phone..." I have already informed all of my clients that you two will be taking over.... Boys just make me proud, make sure you don't allow anything to come between you two.." Duce added as he put the black silk bag containing the diamonds in his top right inside pocket. Both Bossman and myself nodded pretending to be listening whole heartedly, and Duce patted us on our backs as he made his way between us..." Bring those suitcases to the car fellas I gotta get going, I got a midnight flight to catch." Duce said with his back facing us as he walked away.

"Duce...!" I called out as I pulled out my 9mm Smith and Weston and without any care in the world he just turned around slowly. Two shots rang out, one to his leg and the other to his chest then Duce fell to his knees. Neither one of them were a kill shot nor was it my intention to make them one, I walked up to Duce as he was cowardly trying to crawl away on his stomach.

" Aye..... L.A..." He said spitting up blood after I kicked him in his side turning him over to his back before he continued.." What's this all about... Money?" Duce questioned.

"Nah... this ain't about no god damn money... this is for my father..." I answered with so much rage and I watched as his eyes grew bigger.

" Son listen..." he started to say before I interrupted, I brought the barrel of the gun closer to his face. I kneeled down to one knee and placed the pistol underneath his chin.

" I'm not your son..." I said fiercely giving Duce a cold stare into his eyes as I continued..." I had a father and what could have been a perfect family but you... you stripped that away from me.." I stood straight up as I repositioned the pistol to the frontal lobe of his forehead as I posed a question..." Aye..... aye Duce.. All's fair in love and war right..?" I proclaimed as I pulled the trigger and watched as his brain matter splattered all over the concrete then his body fell lifelessly to the ground. I then turned to Bossman who was just about to lite a cigarette..." Aye... help me put him in the trunk..." I said. Bossman walked over and grabbed Duce's limp bottom half as I grabbed the top half. We carried him out to the car and threw him in the trunk of his RR..." Wait here .." I told Bossman as I walked over to my car to grab something and I slowly made my way back over to Bossman and Duce's dead body.

" L.A., man what are you doing..?" Bossman asked as I started pouring gasoline all over the body and the car, I found myself answering what seemed to be a dumb ass question.

" Listen dude, this son of a bitch will die the same way he killed my father.." I declared. Bossman took a few steps back giving a nod of respect or maybe he was just scared I'm not sure, nor did I care. Bossman and I both go back into the warehouse and quickly transferred the suitcases from the warehouse to the trunk of my car then walked back over to the car.

"Wait!" Bossman yelled out stopping me from putting fire to the gas. He walked over and reached inside of Duce's jacket and grabbed the diamonds.." Damn we almost slipped up and forgot these.." he added but upon Bossman's search for the diamonds I noticed that he came across Duces wallet which contained a photo with him, Duce, Monique and their mother in it. Bossman didn't notice that I had my gun in my hand draped down the side of my leg so when he turned around with the diamonds in one hand and the picture in the other, two shots echoed throughout the parking lot.

"I loved you like a brother and cared for you like a friend.... All these years has been nothing but lies and deceit... You betrayed me from the start by hiding the truth and protecting that monster.." I protested. Those two shots pierced through his abdomen causing him to lean against the trunk of the car and making it hard for him to breath. When he finally caught his breath he was only able to utter a few words.

"..... L.A. ... please... you don't have to do this.." he pleaded.

" Bossman.." I said pausing as I felt a warm grin fall upon my face while taking the sack of diamonds from Bossman's hands before I continued... "Its two things throughout my time of knowing you that you taught me..... You taught me the drug game, how to cook it, cut it, and sell it... and I thank you for that street knowledge, you also taught me through this experience to never trust a mutha fucka as far as I can throw them.." I said as I put the pistol to his chest and pulled the trigger, one shot rang out as Bossman's body fell lifelessly into the trunk on top of Duce. I looked at the two bodies once more before walking away from the car giving myself enough distance to light the gas. I lit a cigarette, took one puff and watched as the bodies and the car caught fire. By the time I made it to my car and got in, the car had exploded. I took the diamonds out of my pocket and sat them in the passenger seat along with my gun. I catch a glimpse of myself in the mirror and I see blood all over my shirt, so I took it off and

when I road pass the flaming RR I tossed the shirt into the fire. There was so much going through my mind on my way home and for the first time in a long time in my life I felt at peace. The ride home was the first time I've cried since my father was killed, it hurt but it hurt less knowing that my father's murderer was no longer living. When I got home I took a long extra hot shower and I just sat there on the floor and let the hot water rinse all my pain, frustration, anger, and sadness down the drain.

K.I.M.

Standards

Each individual has their own set of standards that they believe will help them on their quest for love. True some standards help but some standards also hinder your quest for love, because there is such a thing as right and wrong standards to hold a person to. See the thing about standards nowadays is that they are so poisoned by our environment, our past relationships or encounters and more commonly the way we are raised. A child that grows up in an abusive household where daddy beats mommy, if that child isn't mentally strong enough then they break and consequently think that this is how a relationship should be. " That's love". That misguidance ultimately changes the perception or standards for what they look for in a spouse. Eventually you get stuck in the wrong type of love, but do understand that holding an individual to a certain standard means you should hold yourself to that same standard. You can't say " oh, I want someone with goals and ambition" but you don't have either one, or " They gotta have a car.." and you're catching the bus, or " They can't live with their mama.." but you do, or " Someone who won't cheat.." yet you're a habitual cheater, or " Someone who does not have a lot of sex partners." but you're the biggest whore in the city, and my personal favorite.. " I don't want anybody with children" yet you have four of them by four different people. Don't get me wrong someone will always love you for who you are, but my point is if you are holding someone to

certain standards then you should practice what you preach and stick to those same standards you're holding them too. Don't knock someone for their flaws, especially when you may bare the same.

The Long Kiss Good-Night...

I woke up the next morning early enough to catch the news.

" I'm here today on the scene of what law enforcement officers are calling... A senseless act of violence... as you can see behind me we are at an old abandoned Pepsi warehouse where two individuals have been killed and their bodies mutilated by the flames that at one point covered this vehicle. The police say that the two individuals were stuffed inside the trunk of the vehicle, it has not yet been confirmed what the cause of death was, hopefully these individuals didn't suffer by burning alive... The authorities have not yet been able to identify the bodies... As of this moment the police don't have anyone in custody nor has anyone with information come forth, Crime Stoppers is offering a three thousand dollar reward for anyone with information about last night's horrendous crime that leads to an arrest. I am Iisha Henderson with channel eight news reporting to you live from the east side of Darnell City... back to you Richard.." I turned the TV off thinking to myself its going to take them a few weeks to identify those bodies, at least that's how it was with my father. Even though I told the detectives that I was there that night and I know that this was my father, it still took them about three weeks to positively ID him. Now me being so caught up in my thought process the sudden knock at the door kinda startled me, I walked over and opened the door.

" Hey honey, can you help me with my bags..?" Monique asked. Mind you she only has two suitcases but they both had to weigh eighty pounds a piece.

" Damn Baby Girl, I did say pack light.." I said as I snatched the bags off of the front porch and sat them in the hallway by the door while Monique made her way to the kitchen.

" I tried honey but I didn't know what I wanted to wear.." she responded playfully.

" So what you do..?... pack ya whole closet..?" I questioned as we both shared a laugh before Monique opened up the refrigerator.

" No silly.... I just wanted to look special for you.... Anyways did you eat yet?" She asked.

" Whatever you put on will be special enough...-" I said as I walked over to her wrapping my arms around her waist before leaning in closer..." how about we just leave all of that here and when we get there we can go shopping and grab a few things.." I suggested as I whispered into her ear.

" Okay.." she simply responded submissively and I smacked her on her ass as I walked away.

" And No I didn't eat yet.." I replied as I watched her pull out some eggs and milk then placed it on the counter.

" Well by the time you shower and get dressed I'll have something ready for you..." Monique responded before I started taking my shirt off in front of her.

" You coming with..?" I asked teasingly, I caught her biting her bottom lip.

" Nope... we have a flight to catch Mr..." she protested.

" Well if you change ya mind, you know where to find me.." I said as I tossed my shirt over to her and walked away. I got inside the shower and to my surprise she didn't change her mind at all. The whole time I'm in the shower and getting dressed I'm just replaying the events from last night in my head and I couldn't get that image of Bossman's body growing weaker with each shot that ran through him out of my mind.

"Honey are you all set.?... our plane leaves in about an hour.." I heard Monique call out through the halls. I walked into the kitchen and she was putting the finishing touches on my food so I sat down at the table and she brought it over to me..." An omelet with turkey sausage, bell pepper, tomato and onions inside with shredded cheese with basil on top.... eat up.." She said as she sat the plate down next to my orange juice.

"You not eating..?" I asked after taking a bite of the mouth watering omelet.

"Nah, I ate already baby.." Monique answered before turning on the t.v. and it was just my luck that channel eight was showing the same story again and I instantly lost my appetite.

"Wow, it's sad how people nowadays are just killing each other and bringing harm to one another.." She said sadly. I had the urge to quickly defend myself then I remembered that she has no idea what's going.

"Yeah it's messed up that they're dead, but then again you never know what they did to deserve it.." I said as I leaned forward turning off the t.v. before going on.." Anyways my love, are you ready to go...?" I asked and Monique just nodded her head as she leaned in and gave me a kiss.

"Thank you.." She said.

"What exactly are you thanking me for my love..?" I questioned. She placed her right hand on the left side of my face and into my eyes as she spoke.

"For showing me what love truly looks like.." she said.

"I guess we both was looking in the wrong places.." I replied as I wiped from her face a tear that began to run down the side of her cheek and perfected the moment with another kiss. After a few moments of passionately kissing we finally made our way to the front door..." Oh, I almost forgot...-" I reached inside the front closet and grabbed a duffle bag that had a little under seven hundred and fifty thousand dollars

in it, and I reached up top and grabbed another bag relatively smaller than the first.

"What's that?" Monique asked as she pointed at the smaller bag.

"Well it's really none of your business but if you must know it's my special bag, just for you..." I answered and she smiled as she opened the door.

"Mmmm hmm, just for me huh?... so what's in this ""special bag""?" She curiously asked.

"Something for me to know and for you to find out..." I simply said as I placed both bags in the trunk. Most of the ride to the airport Monique was on the phone with her best friend telling her about the trip we were getting ready to take, I wasn't really in tune with the convo but it made me feel good seeing how excited she was about it; and about five minutes away from the airport Monique hangs up and dials another number.

"That's strange.." she said.

"What, what's wrong?" I asked as I glanced over at her.

"I have been trying to reach my brother all morning its not like him to not answer and if he missed my call he would call back... have you talked to him...?" she asked as she looked back at her phone.

"Nah... not today... the last time I heard from him, him and Janel got into a huge argument but knowing him they're probably making up right now.." I said as she quickly covered her ears.

"Oh... thanks for that repulsive image of my brother....thanks a lot..." Monique responded. We laugh as we pull into the car parking area designated to those who are leaving their car while they go on their trips. We made our way through customs patrol and onto the plane with ten minutes to spare before take off.

"L.A...... so just out of curiosity how many other women have you taken on trips like this...?" She asked.

"Just one other woman.." I answered honestly and the slight grin that was on her face slowly disappeared after my response before I went on.." You and my mother " I added then her grin came back as she sat down in her seat next to me laying her head on my shoulder. We both slept throughout the flight, once we got there it was early Friday morning which was a perfect time to do a little shopping. As soon as we got off of the plane and made our way to the lobby I

saw our chauffer for the weekend standing there with a sign above his abdomen that read my name.

" Ah... you must be Mr. L.A. ... welcome to London and to you as well my lady.." the older European man said, he was very polite and showed great hospitality.." May I take your bags sir..?" he questioned.

" Sure.." I said as I handed him the duffle bag and the smaller bag.

" Right this way you two your carriage awaits.." the man said as he walked us to the car and opened our door then loaded the trunk...

" I apologize sir where are my manners, ... my name is William Crawford the third and I will be your driver for the weekend.." William said.

" Its a pleasure to meet you Mr. Crawford..-" I said before he interrupted.

" Please, William is just fine sir." he said.

" Okay William, do we have to check into our rooms right now..?" I asked.

" No sir not here... as long as you have reservations for that day, you just check in whenever you please..." William answered. I checked my watch after looking at the radio in the car to adjust the time since there's a time zone difference. Since my watch read 3:45 am and its a six hour difference between us I set my watch for 9:45 am.

" Well William as you can see we didn't bring much with us, is there any malls nearby we can go to and do a little shopping..." I asked.

" Yes sir.... I know just the place.." William said as he snapped his fingers and started up the car before pulling off. On our way there Monique was busy taking pictures and enjoying the beautiful view of the different buildings and monuments. We pulled up to this place called Ah'veaTor which I later found out from William meant "The Chosen Few". We hop out of the car and while Monique was busy taking selfies in front of the mall I went to the trunk and grabbed about seventy thousand out of the duffle bag. I walked over to William and tried handing him three hundred dollars.

"I'm sorry sir, we do not take tips.." William tried to protest but I just placed the money in his hands.

"William, go and get something nice for yourself.. just meet us back here in about three hours..." I suggested knowing that I wanted to spoil my baby.

"Yes sir,.." William said as he pulled off while Monique and I made our way into the building. I honestly didn't expect for them to have some of the same outlets that we have back home and immediately Monique tries to dip off towards Victoria Secrets.

"Monique.." I called out and she turned around beginning to walk back my way before I went on.." Ima let you do your thang while I go and grab me a few things... so take this and if you run out, give me a call.." I said as I reached into my pocket and gave her thirty two thousand dollars.

"Baby, really I don't need all of this..." she said as she tried handing it back but when she looked at my face she saw how adamant I was towards the motion, so we just agreed to disagree by going our separate ways. My first stop was Lovers Lane to do a little browsing and ended up grabbing a few things to add to my special bag. I took my time as I looked through multiple outlets and boutiques grabbing a few outfits along the way, and my phone hadn't rung so I assumed Monique was doing just fine with her spending. After a while I made my way over to their food court and enjoyed a "Tall" strawberry smoothy though I'm not really sure why they call it "Tall" when its clearly a regular sized cup, while I'm sitting down enjoying my shake my phone goes off.

"Hello.." I answered.

"Hey honey, could you meet me over at the dress boutique across from J.L. Stones..?... I really need your help.." Monique asked as I got up and began to walk in that direction.

"I'll be there in just a minute.." I said and by the time I hung up I was already a little under one hundred feet away from the doors, but even from that distance I could see Monique standing in the window on top of a platform in a beautiful lavender dress that almost matched her beauty. When I made my way into the shop both Monique's beauty and the dress that draped from her shoulders down to about six inches above her knee, grew more elegant. The dress was fitted but not extra tight, it had a slit that started from the V-neck cut of the dress down to about three inches below her breast, which created a perfect separation of her breast.

" So honey, what do you think...?" she questioned as she did a few spins for me but I couldn't help but smile as I admired her beauty.

" I love it..-" I said as I turned to the young lady that was helping Monique out..." She'll take it.." I told the young lady. The young lady looked a little confused as she stood there.

" I'm not sure if you noticed or not sir... but this is a thirty seven thousand dollar dress.." She said. Now maybe it was because I was black or because I was a tourist that the young lady felt the need to inform me about a price but I didn't like it not one bit.

" Trust me babygirl I'm not worried about a price... nor did I ask you for one... So if you were to be so kind and do what it is that you get paid to do which is help the customer and ring a customer up rather than running your mouth, I would greatly appreciate that.." I replied. The young lady stormed off as if I had hit a nerve and Monique began hitting me on my arms trying not to laugh.

" No need to be so mean.." Monique said in a joking manner as she made her way to the dressing room before going on.." I didn't spend that much money I just grabbed me a few outfits, purses, shoes and something a little special for you.... so baby thanks but mama don't

have enough for this dress..." Monique added as I looked over and saw a pile of shopping bags piled up on the sitting area.

" Don't worry about the dress love.... I'll get that for you...?" I responded.

" Thank you baby..." She said as she finally stepped out of the dressing room, then she walked right up to me and planted a kiss on me before going on.." You know you don't have to spoil me to keep me right?..." she asked as I placed my left hand on the right side of her face.

" I know I don't have to.... understand that if I do for you then it's done from the heart because I wanted to.... and because you deserve it..." I explained then she gave me another kiss before helping me haul all of these bags to the front counter. Monique sat the dress she was just modeling down onto the counter as the young lady rang her up.

" That will be thirty seven thousand eight hundred and seventy five dollars oh and eight-teen cent.." the young lady said with a bit of an attitude. I gave the bitch the money and as she's counting me back my change I noticed that they had a little " Tip "jar.

"oh I see you all take tips...." I inquired causing the mood of the young lady to change almost instantly.

" Yes... yes sir we do.." she answered but it was a priceless moment seeing that smile she had on her face go away as I spoke.

" Well I have a tip for you... You should focus more on customer service than worrying about how much money another person has to spend.." I responded and Monique wrapped her arm around mine as we turned to leave the shop. It had been at least three and a half hours that had passed so I was sure that Monique and I would have to haul around all these bags looking for William. To my surprise when we stepped outside he was parked right at the entrance, William jumped out the car and helped put the bags in the trunk.

" You and the lady enjoy your shopping sir..?" he asked as he closed the trunk.

" Yes, I see now why its called The Chosen Few.... everything in there was high end and top of the line..." I responded as I got into the car.

" Yes sir, I figured since you needed to do some shopping you would want some things that are in style..... so where to now sir..?... The hotel..?" William asked.

"Nah, not just yet William... the lady and I would like to see some of the beautiful sites London has to offer.... you know any good places.." I asked as I checked my watch.

" I thought you'd never ask sir..." he replied as he turned around with a grin on his face before pulling off and showing us around the city. He even showed us different monuments that we were able to take pictures in front of, the whole experience was great but not as amazing as the events that were yet to come. Afterwards I finally had William take Monique and I to the hotel, now when I was online I didn't pay much attention to it but seeing it in person it was beautiful.

" The Sysco.... it looks amazing honey.. and it's next to the famous London Bridge.." Monique said as her eyes continued to wonder around then William and a few of the bell boys assisted with taking our bags into the building. Every floor piece and wall was marble, every chandelier was crystal the place was just immaculate

" Hello welcome to Sysco, how can I help you...?" The woman said as Monique and I approached the front desk.

" Yes, I have reservations for L.A. ..." I said as the young lady whose name tag read Ashley typed the name into the computer.

" Ah.... L.A. here you are... we were starting to think that your flight may have been delayed..."

Ashley stated with a thing of curiosity in her voice as to why we were so late.

" Nope, just had to do a little shopping and site seeing.." Monique stepped in and said. Ashley looked over at our cart and slightly giggled.

" *Yeah I see.... well here's your room key card sir, if you need anything just give us a call by pressing star zero one on your room phone and we will happily assist you" Ashley gracefully said as she handed me the card.*

" *Thank you for your hospitality Ashley.." I responded as I took the key then handed it to Monique.*

" *Not a problem sir, these gentlemen will show you to your room... you two enjoy your stay.." Ashley added as we walked off. The men showed us our room and my god was it huge, it was about the size of two major dance studio's.*

" *Oh my god honey.... its perfect.." Monique said as she made her way over to the window to see the view. The men dropped off the bags and departed while I took all that was mine and headed to the bedroom.*

" *I'm about to hop in the shower first, then its all yours.... I told William to meet us back here in two hours..-" I said as I turned the shower on.*

" *Why, where are we going..?" Monique rudely interrupted to ask.*

" *Now if I told you.... it wouldn't be a secret now would it...?" I sarcastically questioned.*

" *How will I know what to wear...?" she asked.*

" *That dress that I bought you baby will do just fine...." I answered as I went ahead and took me*

a nice shower, got dressed and waited for Monique to get herself together but I ended up dosing off on the sofa then I heard a voice.

" *How do I look...?" she asked. I wasn't sure if my eyes were deceiving me or not but she looked more beautiful now than before. She had her hair pinned up, the lavender dress on with a pair of lavender ankle strap high heels to top it off and her aroma was very enticing as well.*

" *You..... you look magnificent... wow..." I said as my eyes just couldn't stop admiring her beauty, nor would they allow me to stop visually stripping her.*

" Thank you... you clean up good yourself, you should wear suits more often.." She said as she fixed my tie, then we made our way outside.

" Sir... Madam..." William said greeting us as he opened our doors, once inside the car William continued... "Where to sir..?"

"Do you know where Bridgeton Olivettee is...?" I questioned.

"Why yes I do... its actually not too far, I'll have you there in a jiff..." William said wasting no time responding. William was right we had fifteen minutes until our reservations kicked in and he got us there in about ten minutes..." here we are sir.." William added before he parked the car and came around to open Monique's door.

" This is beautiful L.A...." Monique said as she looked around and those were the only words she could muster up as we stepped into the building.

" Good evening my name is Rhonda, welcome to Bridgeton Olivettee.... I'll be your host for tonight, will you be inside or outside dinning this evening..?" The young lady asked and I looked around for a quick moment in disbelief that this is only a four star restaurant when it should be a five star.

"Ah... I'm not really sure, I just have reservations for two..." I said.

"Name?.." she questioned.

"L.A. ...." I simply responded then Rhonda checked the clipboard.

" Ah... here you are, if you would be so kind as to follow me right this way your table is ready..-" She said as she walked us over to our table.." your server will be with you shortly..." she said before departing. Shortly after Rhonda left the server walked up and the sweet young lady took our order and brought us some drinks while we waited on our food. Before our food came Monique and I started engaging in deep conversation, and even after our food was gone hours later we still found ourselves talking.

"What do you think about us..?" I asked.

" I think we are good all by ourselves.... but you and I are a greater force when we're together...-" she said pausing for a moment to allow

*what she had just said to sink in before going on.." what about you..?"
She countered.*

" Well, I fully agree with you but I also think that we are in a perfect place, at the perfect time, enjoying a perfect meal with someone I believe to be the perfect woman..." I answered as she leaned across the table in a seductive manner.

" Oh yeah, well don't that mean we need a perfect ending to a perfect night..?" Monique questioned.

" I agree..... so what is it that you had in mind..?" I asked then she sat back in her seat with a smile on her face as she called for the server.

" Check please...." she said before turning her attention to me before going on..." I'm sure we can think of a few things..." she added as the check came and she insisted on paying, so I let her. We got in the car and went right back to the hotel, I stopped over at the front desk as Monique grabbed the elevator.

"Hey.." I said.

" Yes sir, how can I help you...?" the young man asked.

" I need you to have a bottle of wine, a bucket of ice and a full plate of fresh cut strawberries up to room 811 as soon as possible..." I answered leaning in close so that Monique couldn't hear me.

" Right away sir.." the young man responded as he grabbed the phone.

" Thank you..." I said as I gracefully made my way over to the elevator with Monique. As soon as the doors closed she jumped all over me kissing and touching. We made it up to the room and her aggression intensifies, she pushed me up against the door while kissing me and undoing my shirt before stopping.

" I'll be right back.... stay dressed..." she said as she ran towards the bathroom and meanwhile I fish out my special bag and sit it on the night stand next to the bed, then there's a knock at the door. When I opened the door it was one of the kitchen boys with a silver cart that held wine, ice and some strawberries. I rolled the cart in and gave him a tip then took the items and placed them on the night stand before I

laid across the bed, moments later I hear her voice…. "I know you're not going to sleep on me…?" she questioned. I sat up and my jaw dam near dropped to the floor when I saw her standing there in a lavender sheer laced panty and bra set. Her skin was so smooth, she climbed on top of me and our lips touched and I can tell by the way that she's kissing me that she's trying to take control. Key word being "trying", we ended up switching positions and I pinned her down to the bed as I whispered in her ear with a soft tone.

" Close your eyes.." I demanded and without any hesitation she quickly complied. I reached into my special bag and pulled out a blindfold and placed it on her, so now that I don't have to worry about her peeking I continue.." Give me your hands .." I said as I reached into my special bag again and grabbed two pairs of handcuffs. I cuffed one pair to the bed connecting it to the pair of cuffs I just placed on her wrist. I then removed the blindfold I figured it would be more of a tease for her to watch what comes next and not be able to touch. I grabbed the strawberries off of the nightstand and placed them on the bed next to her then I fed Monique a few slices before I started placing them all over her body. There was only a select few spots that I wanted to put strawberries, so when I was done with that portion I started slowly eating them off of her. As I am following the trail of strawberries I noticed that I was leaving kiss marks and hicky's all over her neck, chest, stomach and her inner thighs. It seems like the closer I get to her pussy the wetter she becomes, I can even see the juices running down her leg and trust me its not from the strawberries. I come back up just to whisper in her ear " I love you.." before making my way back down, but before I continue with my pursuit I grabbed a handful of strawberries and placed them on the lips of her pussy I maintain eye contact with her and start devouring her warm, juicy pussy even after all the strawberries are gone because my main focus is to please her and from the sound of her continuous moaning and multiple orgasms I must be doing good. I wrapped her legs around my

neck sinking my nails into her thighs while my tongue is continuously making love to her juicy pussy lips as well as her clit. As I continue sucking and licking on her clit I can feel it starting to swell up which tells me that more than likely she's getting ready to release a fat one, so before she climaxes I start doing little tricks with my tongue that simply drives her crazy. Trying her best to run she couldn't go far being cuffed up and all, and I looked up at her as I'm still devouring her pussy and she has a look in her eyes as if she can't take it anymore. I watch as her eyes roles in the back of her head and her legs start to shake uncontrollably, so I used my tongue to press up against her clit as she came.

" Baby...... ooo baby I love you..." Monique moaned out all out of breath so I decided to uncuff her as I took my time cleaning up the mess I left running from her pussy down her inner thigh, and the whole time that her hands are free she begins caressing my head and pulling my hair. By this time I done made my way back up to her neck before she rolls over, now she's on top of me. Monique finishes undressing me and slowly starts kissing me all over my neck down to my chest then I feel her grab my dick and rub it against her clit, and we both let out a moan or relief as she eases down on top of it. She places her hands on my chest and starts slowly rocking back and forth while we're kissing, I let her ride and relax for a few moments then I had to get back to my mission which was to make sure Monique has the best night of her life. I sit up easing her off of me before getting up and guiding her over to the dresser where I turned her around so that she can see me through the mirror. I grip her waist with both hands and she bends over creating the most perfect arch in her back, then I smack Monique on her ass as I slide my dick inside of her. I look up in the mirror and catch her rolling her eyes and biting down on her bottom lip as I continue to ease my way inside of her.

" You like that huh...?" I asked finding it almost funny that when she tried to answer she couldn't, so she just settled for nodding her head

for confirmation to the question. The sound of my balls smacking against the lips of her wet juicy pussy and her moaning only encouraged me to go faster. The faster I went the harder each stroke was, and the harder each stroke was the deeper she could feel my dick inside her. It was crazy how quick I went from making love to trying to fuck the life out of her. I wrapped one hand around her waist and the other tightly around her neck, and as I slowed up the strokes I continued kissing sucking and biting all over her neck and ear. I can feel her using her pussy muscles trying to make me tap out because she can't take any more, so I pull out. When I pull out Monique turned around and kisses me as I softly bite down on her bottom lip. Monique guided me into the bathroom where once inside she pushed me up against the door and started stroking my dick, and when I started to speak she simply placed her index finger across my lips as she started kissing me on my neck working her way down. She looks up at me as she's holding my dick in her hands and started licking the tip of it slow and very seductively. Once she saw me biting my lip she started going to work, slobbing and spitting all over my shit as I watched and after a few moments I brought her back up to eye level before sitting her on the sink.

" I'll be right back..." I said as I ran back out into the room grabbed a few ice cubes then returned. I placed the two ice cubes in my mouth and started running it from her neck down to her chest, down to her stomach and the closer I got to her pussy the quicker the ice starts to melt so I kept running my lips with the ice across the lips of her pussy until it melts. After she climaxes she gets down off the sink and turns on the shower before getting in then I follow behind. With her back pressed against the wall she begins kissing me and as soon as I started kissing back I felt her arms wrap around my neck and her legs around my waist.

" Give it to me baby..." She moaned out as I rammed my dick deep inside of her constantly pounding harder and harder. Monique sunk

her teeth into my neck as she tried to keep from screaming so loud and when I was ready to cum she could tell, she could feel the difference in my strokes.... "I know you're about to cum baby... don't pull out!..... and don't stop!" Monique demanded as she held my face in the palm of her hands looking into my eyes. Now had this been any other woman I would have stopped right then or at least pulled out, but Monique wasn't any other woman so therefore I respected her wishes. When I felt myself getting ready to cum to start giving her long deep strokes while she was sinking her nails into my back. We made eye contact right before I nutted and when it shot inside of her we both let out a loud moan of satisfaction, and we shared a few more kisses before I finally let her down.

"You can go lay down honey, I'll be there in just a second.." she said and that's exactly what I did, taking advantage of the alone time I grabbed the last item out of my special bag and placed it under her pillow. By the time she made it into the room I was half sleep and we both were fully undressed, she got under the cover with me and laid across my chest.

"That, was amazing..." I said as I kissed her on her forehead.

"No..... it was perfect.." she rebutted. I laid there playing through her hair and I couldn't help but to think to myself how I have my family, money, and the woman of my dreams someone that really completes me, what else could I possibly need?. I pulled out the box from underneath her pillow and opened it in front of Monique.

"............... Will you Marry me..?..............."

UNITED

My heart is racing, The room is beginning to spin
My palms are sweaty, When will this journey end?
My eyes are red and puffy I can barely stand
I'm trying to hold on to reality
Piece by piece slip through my hands
I can't stop pacing , My breathing gets fierce
My ears are aching, Not long before tears appear
My knees go weak
But I gotta stay strong
because it won't be long
Before you'll be coming home.

The End

Thank You!!!!

If you made it this far then again, I appreciate you believing in me, thank you for reading the book and thank you for supporting the movement.

**Be sure to answer the following questions and submit your answers to receive 5$ off your next order.*

1. Who was your favorite character? Why?

2. How do you feel about how L.A handled the situation with Duce and Bossman?

3. What would you have liked to have seen more of in this book?

4. What do you anticipate book 2 (E.S.C.A.P.E.) to be like.

5. Which character BEST describes you? Why?

E.S.C.A.P.E.

(Eventually Sex will Cripple A Persons Emotions)

Love has the potential to be the best thing that has ever happened to you, and in that same breath become your worst nightmare. Only when the love starts to become toxic does the relationship begin to spiral downhill.... True when you love someone you don't just give up when the going gets tough, but when you don't know when to cut your losses and walk away then you become trapped in an unhealthy relationship. The one thing that holds together 1 out of every 3 relationships is sex, and because the relationship was built off of physical chemistry sex becomes the only aspect of the relationship they both enjoy. " Well what about the toxic relationships that aren't bounded together by sex?" Have you ever held ya breath against someone and when you started to gasp for air you held in a little longer because you didn't want to be the first one to give up?... Well that same resistance to being the first one to give in is the same reason why a lot of people are stuck in toxic relationships today. When you love someone sometimes its hard to let go, but you have to... in the best interest of yourself; because at the end of the day your happiness is key so you have to pull away..... "But what happens when its too late to ESCAPE?"..

Don't miss out!

Visit the website below and you can sign up to receive emails whenever Im Him publishes a new book. There's no charge and no obligation.

https://books2read.com/r/B-A-FQLW-WYJEC

BOOKS2READ

Connecting independent readers to independent writers.

About the Author

L.A. is a young Detroit native. The oldest out of 3 to a single mother who was the sole provider due to the loss of her husband. L.A. was young when he loss his father, inhibiting his opportunity to fully experience his childhood. This tragic loss was just one stone that contributed to L.A's strong mental foundation. The obstacles to face along the road were nothing short of calamitous, but one of the biggest obstacles was the loss of his daughter. L.A. took that event and turned it into L.O.V.E. He used this series not only as an initial distraction; but to leave a legacy by providing a glimpse into his life, and the things that cultivated him into the man he is today.

www.ingramcontent.com/pod-product-compliance
Lightning Source LLC
Chambersburg PA
CBHW060918140726
47996CB00001B/295